FIND THE MONEY

The mysterious Vanessa has vanished, and it's worth a million dollars to a vicious drug lord to get her back. But the ransom disappears, turning up in the hands of a bewildered innocent bystander, while ruthless gangsters and hapless kidnappers alike desperately search for the money. Meanwhile, Detective Marlon Morrison, who only wants to comfortably ride out the final year and a half before his retirement without incident, finds himself involved with a growing succession of murder victims, and a bizarre case growing in complexity by the hour . . .

TONY GLEESON

FIND THE MONEY

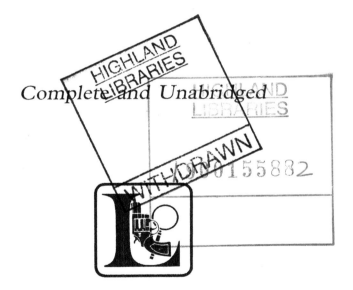

Complete and Unabridged

LINFORD
Leicester

First published in Great Britain

First Linford Edition
published 2020

A catalogue record for this book is available
from the British Library.

ISBN 978–1–4448–4374–3

Published by
F. A. Thorpe (Publishing)
Anstey, Leicestershire

Set by Words & Graphics Ltd.
Anstey, Leicestershire
Printed and bound in Great Britain by
T. J. International Ltd., Padstow, Cornwall

This book is printed on acid-free paper

DEDICATION:
To Costas, the translator

Prologue

How much space does a million dollars take up?

All United States bills, from the one-dollar bill all the way up to the ten thousand, are of uniform size: to be precise, 6.14 inches long, 2.61 inches wide, and .0043 of an inch thick. Doing a little basic math, this means that one million dollars in U.S. $100 bills would nestle nicely, in 100 stacks of 100 bills, in a shallow carton about a foot and a half square, with some breathing space left. All in all, less than half a cubic foot, weighing a touch over 22 pounds.

Perhaps surprisingly, so little storage space for so much money.

For most of us, this is nothing more than a simple intellectual exercise, and probably a tedious and irrelevant one at that; but there was at least one person for whom this was a quite meaningful problem.

That wasn't his only problem.
But let's not get ahead of ourselves.

1

There were many reasons why Yancey Rybus had risen to the summit of a wildly successful, well-structured enterprise. He had a sharp business sense and a talent for organization. He believed in equal opportunity, employing and rewarding those who could demonstrate their ability to finance and protect his operation, regardless of their background or former affiliation.

But clearly the cardinal factor in his stellar success was fear, of the gut-wrenching variety. Yancey Allan Rybus ran the illegal drug trade in his city: all of it, for the entire greater metropolitan area.

He instilled chilling terror into the soul of every single person with whom he dealt. He never lost his temper. His constant, calm equanimity had a quality more dreadful than any temper display ever could have.

He was not known to hold grudges,

mostly because his 'problems' seldom lasted long enough to cause them to arise.

For these reasons, the young man named Darius now sitting before Yancey Rybus was more terrified than he had ever been before.

Generally, only the boss's most trusted lieutenants got to sit with him at this walnut table in his private office, above the nightclub that fronted his operation. But now and then, he would invite one of his underlings to this exclusive venue to have a little conversation.

If you were an underling, it was whispered, this was never a good thing.

Rybus sat back in a large leather chair, elbows resting on the padded armrests, fingers laced, staring placidly through his stylish tinted glasses. Standing in brooding silence next to him, arms folded, dressed in a black open-neck shirt and pants, was the largest human being Darius had ever known. He was a perfect example of Rybus's commitment to diversity, a Samoan by the name of Sylvester Faamoana. After an abortive attempt at a career in professional football and wrestling, Sylvester had found a happier fit for his unique talents. He was now Rybus's irreplaceable special assistant, known to everyone in the crew simply as Tiny.

'So tell me one more time, Darius, my lad, just how you managed to lose my dear Vanessa? Leave nothing out.'

Darius nervously scratched at the new bright blue tattoo along the side of his neck. It still itched; in fact, right now he felt crawly everywhere.

'I'm sorry, Mr. Rybus. I was keeping an eye on her, I really was, like I always do on our Sunday morning walks. I wasn't letting her out of my sight, not for a moment. Just like you always told me, she could go where she wanted but with me keeping an eye on her. What happened was, like, a quirk. We were on Croftworth, that street over by the university; you know how much she likes to walk over there, on a nice sunny day like today, with all those beautiful trees and the flowers she loves to smell? And this old drunk or whatever just came out of nowhere, stumbling down the street with a bunch of, like, boxes in his arms.'

'The boxes. Mm-hmm.'

'So I made sure we moved over out of the guy's way because he didn't seem quite right, but when he got close, he suddenly tripped or something and fell right into me. The damned boxes went everywhere. I fell over too. I immediately got to my feet, Mr. Rybus. *Immediately.* I pushed the guy outa the way and looked around. She was gone!'

'Gone. Just like that.'

'I was on the outside of the walk, the traffic side. She had to have gone onto the campus, through the trees and bushes. I ran in there and looked everywhere, calling out her name over and over. There was nothing.'

Rybus nodded quietly. 'And the . . . drunk?'

'When I got back, he was gone. Left the boxes all over the ground. I figured out it had to have been a snatch.'

Rybus cleared his throat meaningfully. 'Smart boy.'

'I searched up and down the street for the guy. Nothing.'

'It took you a while to call in about this, though, didn't it?'

For Darius, the mere act of swallowing right now was an effort. In his mind, he ran through those jaw-clenching minutes that had seemed like hours as he frantically ran back and forth, realizing Vanessa was gone and he was in deep trouble. He formulated what his story was going to be to save his own neck: it had to have been a dedicated snatch, planned out by a team with organization and brains behind it. He had to paint himself as the victim. He had to make the boss see that this could have happened to anybody.

'I . . . what I mean is, I . . . wanted to see if I could find Vanessa or the guy before I hit the panic button.'

'Hmm. We wouldn't want you to panic, now, would we?'

'Really, I went everywhere all up and down the street, stopped everyone I saw, described Vanessa and asked if they'd seen her. I didn't want to alarm you unnecessarily. You know, there're times

7

she likes to sneak off on her own. She likes to play those kinds of games with me.'

'Oh, I'm sure she does. That's why I chose somebody I figured I could trust to not let her *play those games* on them. Someone like you.'

'I'm sorry, Mr. Rybus. You know I've never let you down before. If this is some kind of a snatch, this coulda happened to anyone.'

Rybus nodded thoughtfully.

'What did this fellow look like, this apparent drunk with the . . . boxes?'

'It happened so fast. He was tall, maybe six feet or more. He had a hat pulled down over the top of his head, one of those wool caps, and some kinda coat. Something long and dark. I couldn't see it all that well. Because of the boxes, you know?'

'The boxes. Yes.'

'He had armloads of 'em. Wait, now that I think about it, I did notice one thing: he was a ginger.'

'A ginger? What . . . ?'

'You know. His hair was kinda red.

What was sticking out from under the cap, I mean. And . . . yeah, I'm pretty sure he had some kind of beard. That was sorta red too.' Darius hesitated for a long, uncomfortable beat. 'Or . . . maybe it was just his face was red.'

Rybus sighed with immense patience. 'Anything else you noticed about him?'

'He kinda smelled bad.'

'Did he speak?'

'He kinda muttered, like a wino. His voice was all raspy, like he was maybe trying to disguise it.'

'And what was in the boxes?'

Darius hesitated. 'Uh . . . from what I saw, they all looked empty.'

There was a long interval of dead silence. Darius was sure they all could hear his heart pounding. He finally had to say something.

'It coulda happened to anybody, Mr. Rybus. They took me by surprise.'

Rybus nodded, looking a little sad. He sighed. 'But it happened to you, Darius, my lad, didn't it?' He raised his right hand and gestured casually toward Tiny. The big man instinctively knew what that meant. So, unfortunately, did Darius, who began whimpering pitifully even as Tiny stepped forward, wrapped an enormous hand around the smaller man's bicep, firmly pulled him from the chair and led him to a side door.

'Don't worry,' Rybus said to him as he was escorted away. 'Tiny's just going to ask you a few more questions, just to make sure that your story's one hundred percent *accurate*. That you didn't forget anything.'

It was tacitly understood all around that, after his little debriefing, Darius would not be returning to work.

Darius's pleading faded away as the door closed behind them. Rybus sat still in the room by himself, deep in thought. Finally he removed his glasses with one hand and wiped a small tear from the corner of his eye with the other.

'Vanessa,' he whispered, shaking his head, 'not gonna lose you too. Don't worry, baby, I'm gonna get you back. Whatever it takes.'

★ ★ ★

There were not many people who had earned Yancey Rybus's confidence sufficiently to rise to his inner circle, and they had to constantly work to hold that precarious faith. His most trusted lieutenant had been with him for many years, in which time he had demonstrated his ability to take care of whatever needed to be addressed. For that reason within the organization he was not generally known by his given name, which was Theo, but by his initials, T.C. To speak to Rybus it was necessary to first go through T.C., and that was why the two men now sat across from one another in a far more amicable meeting at the same boss's table.

'This was just delivered in a box with your name on it,' Theo said, placing a cell phone on the table between them. 'They've made contact. A burner, probably bought at some store out of town. They sent a text from another burner.'

Rybus picked up the phone and thumbed through to the messages. Theo remained calm but held his breath. Yancey was not going to like this. There was nothing in the world that mattered more to him than Vanessa, maybe not even their intricate and immensely profitable operations. This whole thing was a major distraction, and not at a good time. There were delicate negotiations going on, shipments anticipated, cash payments being accumulated and bundled, schedules for cutting and distributing of new product to be arranged, and all this on top of the regular collection routines. This was going to complicate things a whole lot. He watched as his boss scrolled through the text message. 'They say she's all right. For now. They sent a photo.'

Rybus nodded. 'They want a million, huh? One million. In hundreds.' His expression remained placid but Theo could feel the storm building inside the man. They were hitting him where he lived and there would be sheer hell to pay. 'Hundreds. Very specific.'

'What do you want me to do?'

'Get it together. It says they'll contact me later with the details.'

'You're gonna do it?'

'Of course I'm going to do it. But that's not all I'm going to do.'

Theo nodded.

'Text from an out of state area code. Probably a faked caller ID anyway.' Rybus held the phone up. 'I'm guessing they figure there's no way we can trace them from this?'

'Likely not. But I'll look into it very closely.'

'You do that. Think these guys are pros?'

'I'm not sure. They're organized. They thought this out. Could be some serious people we're up against.'

'They might be, but what they've decided to do is very stupid.'

Theo ran the possibilities through his mind. Things had been quiet lately. Not long ago the city's drug business had been divided up among several outfits, each generally keeping to their own territory and maintaining a fragile peace that often came unraveled. Rybus, a master of both the carrot and the stick, had gradually expanded his own operations across the metro area, absorbing or displacing his competition. A single authority meant reasonable peace . . . and thriving business. There hadn't even been a need for much muscle in recent times; mostly internal discipline of a minor rebellion here or there, the kind of thing Tiny could take care of without much bother.

Did this signal a rise of a new competitor, inside or out of the organization, making a play?

Rybus interrupted his train of thought. 'Well, first thing is to get Vanessa back safely. That's most important. How soon can we raise the money?'

They both knew it wouldn't be a huge problem. They often needed to put together large sums of money in large bills, and in fact, anticipating pending transactions, they had already accumulated more than the amount in question. It would only be a matter of making a few visits and leaving a few orders. It would cause deliveries to be postponed, and that would present difficulties. Their money supply was large, but it was limited; they couldn't really afford to have that money out of their pocket for very long. This was a particularly bad time for this whole thing to be happening. It was a delicate subject that Theo knew better than to raise with his boss, not with Vanessa's safety in the balance.

Still, the assumption was that the money would not be out of their hands very long in any case. Nobody was going to be allowed to get away with this. It would be dealt with in earnest and in short order.

Theo stood up. 'Not long. I'll get things going right away.'

'Then we get these people, all of them. And the money back.'

'We will, you can be sure of that.'

Rybus picked up the phone again. 'How did this get here, exactly?'

'It was dropped off with Morty at the bar. Plain cardboard box, just had your name written on it.'

'See what he remembers about who-ever left it with him.' He gestured with the phone. 'I'll hang on to this in the meantime. Stay in close touch.'

Theo nodded and turned toward the

stairs. Something else was particularly troubling to him: whoever had made the grab of Vanessa seemed to know that they could get their hands on a large sum in hundreds quickly. They also seemed to understand just how important Vanessa was to Rybus, that she was his weak link.

The more he thought about it, the more he was convinced this was an inside job. And that would be a *real* problem.

He reached the bottom of the staircase that opened into the club and crossed over to the bar. Morty Moriarty, behind the bar, was the person whose name was on the title to the Hometown Club. He was the perfect front: clean record, no demonstrable connections to organized crime of any kind. A public proprietor like Morty meant no problems owning a bar and getting a liquor and cabaret license for the club. He kept a low profile, went along with the program, and kept completely away from anything of an illegal nature. Rybus, of course, was the real owner, and the Hometown Club was the most important home base for his enterprises.

The Hometown Cub was known among many detectives in Vice, Narcotics, and the Personal Crimes Unit, but nobody had ever been able to find a clear link to Yancey Rybus, as hard as they tried or as frustrated as they became.

Theo sidled up to a quiet stretch of the bar and motioned Morty over. 'The kid who brought that package in . . . what do you remember about him?'

'Young kid. Maybe eight or ten. I dunno, I'm not real good at judging ages. Blue and orange T-shirt with some kinda monster on it. Glasses.'

'Glasses, huh?'

'Yeah. Don't remember much more about him. Don't remember seeing him before. The T-shirt stood out in my mind.'

'So all he did was walk into the club? You guys let a minor just stroll into here?'

'It's early. Almost nobody here. None of the bouncers were on station. He was a little guy, about yay high.' He held his hand around his chest. 'I suddenly saw him and right away told him he couldn't come in here. That's when he held up the box and brought it to me. Said something

17

like, 'I'm supposed to leave this here for the man whose name is on the box.' And he put it on the bar and turned and ran out. He looked scared. I yelled to him but he was out the door like a rabbit. At first I was worried it was, like, a bomb or something. But it was just that little box, you saw it, with one word on the wrapping: Rybus. That's when I called you.'

'Think the kid might still be around?'

Morty shrugged.

Theo walked out of the club and looked up and down the block. He doubted the kid was one of their juvies who sold their product on the corners; that was forbidden within several blocks of the club. Probably just a local kid who happened to be walking by.

Luck seemed to be with him. A block up and across the street, he saw a young boy in a bright blue and orange shirt in front of an ice cream store. He started walking towards the kid, not looking at him, acting nonchalant. As he passed the kid, he shot a look across the street at him: he looked to be about ten, was working intently on a huge ice cream cone, and his bright blue shirt did indeed bear an orange picture of Frankenstein's monster. He looked intelligent, but kind of nerdy. Theo crossed the street at the next intersection and strolled back, paying no attention to him. He could sense the kid tensed up when he passed him but was satisfied that Theo had no interest in him.

He turned just as he passed him and laid a hand on the kid's shoulder. 'Hey, li'l man, what's up?'

The kid about jumped and looked to be ready to run, but Theo pressed on his shoulder a little tighter. 'No need to worry, I'm not gonna do anything to you. I just want to ask you about when you went into the club a while back?'

'What you talking about? I wasn't in there!' He was trying to be brave but his voice was breaking. Theo smiled and nodded his head.

'Come on, now. You know who I am?'

The boy nodded gravely, his eyes wide over the ice cream. Theo figured he was typed as one of the guys the other kids talked about in hushed tones and the parents called the Bad Men he should stay away from.

'All right, then. What's your name, son?'

'Jerome.'

'Okay, Jerome. I know you didn't do anything wrong. Somebody asked you to bring that box in to the bartender, am I right?'

'He gave me a twenty. All I had to do was walk in and hand it to the man at the bar.'

'All right, then. I'd say you made a pretty good deal for yourself. My advice? Don't spend it all on ice cream. All I want is for you to help me out a little bit here. What can you tell me about the guy who gave you the box and the money? Was it just one guy?'

Jerome was quiet, trying to decide if he should answer the question truthfully. Theo's finely wrought mixture of charm and intimidation won out.

'Yeah. Just the one guy.'

'What'd he look like?'

'White dude. Couldn't see him very

well. He had shades and a hat and a hoodie pulled over his head.'

'A hat and a hoodie? It's gotta be in the seventies out here right now. By the way, that cone's starting to drip, better keep working on it while we talk.' The kid took several quick licks all around. 'Tell me more.'

'Like I said, he was all covered up. Big mirrored shades. He kinda looked like the Wolfman.'

'How do you mean? Like he had a beard?'

'Yeah. Whiskers and frizzy hair stickin' out from under the hat. All red hair. What I could see of his face was red too, 'specially his nose. Looked like an asteroid, all bumpy.'

Theo had to smile. 'So, where were you when he stopped you and where'd he come from?'

Jerome pointed down the street toward the club. 'I was walkin' home and he just sorta was there all of a sudden. I guess he came from across the street. He stepped in front of me and said, 'Hey kid, wanta make twenty dollars?' Then he handed me the box and said, 'All you gotta do is take this into that club there and hand it to the man behind the bar. Okay?' I was a little scared but he handed me the twenty, so I figured it was worth it.'

Theo smiled at the boy. 'Pretty brave. So what'd his voice sound like?'

'It was all gruff, like the Wolfman. Like maybe he was pretend talkin'.'

'Uh huh. What'd he do after that?'

'I don't know. I stopped in front of the door for a moment and I was worried, so I looked back at him. But he was gone. I don't know where he went.'

'All right, young man. You did nothing wrong. You're from around here, right?'

Jerome looked suspiciously at Theo for a long moment. 'You're not gonna go talk to my mom, are you? 'Cause she'd kill me if she knew I went in that place.'

Theo smiled his most charming smile. 'No, I'm not going to talk to anybody. But your mom's right. Stay away from there.' The kid nodded. Theo pointed up the street, away from the club. 'Now you better get home.'

After the kid skittered away, Theo ran it

all through his head. It fit with the guy who had distracted that moron Darius and set up the snatch of Vanessa to begin with. Wild red hair, sunglasses, dressed like a bum. This would require some more thought. In the meantime, he needed to start making the rounds to get the money lined up, and dropping a few more delicate questions along the way.

★   ★   ★

Lydia waited for the three-two knock on the door before slowly opening it. When she saw it was Brick, she unlatched the chain and allowed him to enter.

'How'd it go?'

'Fine. I found a kid on the street to bring it in and watched from a distance until I saw him hand it to the bartender. Then I got out of there right away.'

'Are you sure nobody saw you?'

'Sure I'm sure.' He glared at her as if the comment offended him.

'Hey, I'm just being careful.'

'I stayed in the doorway and kept an eye out. Nobody else was on the street.

23

There was hardly anybody in the bar. The kid dropped the box and got out of there fast. By the time anyone would have registered what was going on and come out to take a look, I was gone.'

'What if that kid decides to drop a dime on you? What if he's one of the neighborhood dealers?'

'The kid was, like, nine!'

'And how old do you think they are when they get started on the corners?'

'Aw . . . he didn't strike me that way.'

Lydia rolled her eyes. She increasingly doubted her wisdom in teaming up with Brick.

'He looked like a kinda nerdy kid,' Brick continued. 'And you said the dealer kids aren't allowed to hang out around there anyway. I doubt he could ID me if he wanted to. I had my hat pulled down, my hood up and my shades down.'

'And the temperature's close to 80 today? I bet that didn't look too suspicious.'

'Look, we decided this was the best way to do it, didn't we? I had the element of surprise. It was bold. Nobody would have expected me to go right to his headquarters.'

Lydia shook her head, hands on hips. 'I hope so.'

'And yes, I made sure nobody trailed me back. The car was a few blocks away. Nobody was following me on the street or when I drove away. Look, don't freak out. This is gonna work. He's going to think this is the work of somebody big, some other organization. We'll be lost on the ground, under the radar.'

Under the radar. He certainly liked that expression. She shook her head again. 'I'll be glad when this is over.'

'Me too. Hang in there. How's she doing?' He pointed towards a closed door leading to the back bedroom.

Her face notably softened and the scowl turned to a smile. 'She's a real sweetheart. I think we hit it off; she seems to trust me. She wants to go home, of course. I keep assuring her nothing's going to happen to her and she'll be going home real soon.'

'I hope you're right.'

It amazed Brick that Lydia, a fearsome

woman in so many ways, had such a sweet and tender side when it came to their captive. In general he found her tough and downright scary — lean, muscular, covered with tattoos — but he had to admit, that was also why he found her so attractive and *intriguing*. Undoubtedly that was a big reason her former boyfriend had been so taken with her as well.

No. He did not want to think about him. That was a whole different level of scary.

'We are *not* going to do anything to her.' Lydia stared ferociously at Brick, as if she suspected his intentions towards Vanessa.

He held his hands up in placation. 'Neither of us wants anything to happen to her. But if he refuses to pay?'

'That's not going to happen. He'll pay anything to get her back. Trust me.'

'But just saying. What if he doesn't pay?'

'Then we . . . drop her as planned and run like hell, I guess. But that's not going to happen.'

'We're going to run like hell anyway, as soon as we got the money.'

'As soon as we drop her off. Everything's ready, right?'

'Plane tickets all set. We drive down the coast to La Costilla and hide out until the flight next week. I got my friend set up to launder the money for us and set up safe accounts.'

'And you're sure we can trust this guy?'

'He wouldn't rip us off or cross us; his reputation is on the line. He makes his living off of the percentage for his services. Within a week, our bank accounts are solid, we fly away. We'll have plenty of time. How long will it take them to get the money together?'

'He's got it right now. They put this kind of money together for cash deals all the time, like the one coming up. If he says he can't do it by tomorrow, he's stalling and we up the pressure.'

Brick had to trust her on this. She was the one who knew the organization's ins and outs. His job was the logistics of the payoff itself. He kept telling himself this wasn't all that different from things he had done before and that he knew he was good at.

The difference, he tried *not* to keep telling himself, was that this time he was in the big leagues, dealing with truly dangerous characters. A misstep meant unthinkably worse consequences.

There were a lot of things he preferred not to think about right now. It was better to concentrate on the prize.

The phone, lying on an end table, started to buzz. They both stared at it before she nervously picked it up and tapped the screen a few times.

'He's acknowledging receipt and waiting further instructions. So far so good.' She looked at Brick. 'You're sure there's no way he can trace this phone?'

'We've been over this. He can't.'

'But are you absolutely sure? There's no way they can find us here?'

'No way. Stop worrying.'

'You know when I'll stop worrying? When you bring home the money and we're on our way out of the country. Are you sure about the drop-off point you talked about?'

'I don't see how it could go wrong. I checked it out. It's absolutely perfect. There are no homes or other buildings for a few blocks, and after the park closes, the street is totally deserted. It'll be possible to see anybody waiting or following me. I did my research, trust me.'

What Brick did not mention to Lydia was that his original brainstorm for the drop-off location had come from the uniform he saw on a guy who lived on their street: some kind of park worker for the Aquatic Bird Sanctuary Park. That's when he decided to investigate the area. He noticed a note of skepticism creeping into her comments about his plans. He figured it was better to confidently maintain an aura of mystery around them as best he could.

2

Monday morning, when Theo answered the summons, Rybus was sitting at his usual table, scowling at the cell phone in front of him.

'I got the call. They sent more pictures of her as well.'

Theo dropped into the chair across from him. 'How's she look? Is she okay?'

Rybus swiveled the phone around and pushed it across the table. 'She looks okay. Doesn't look like they've mistreated her and she doesn't look scared. So we might let them die without too much pain when this is over.'

Theo scrolled through the photos, making note of details in the background that might come in handy, and read the message aloud. It was all in capitals, as if the sender were shouting. 'PLACE MONEY IN STACKS OF $100 BILLS IN A PLAIN BLACK TRASH BAG. LEAVE UNDERNEATH BENCH ON

LAKE DRIVE AND BARLOW AT AQUATIC BIRD SANCTUARY AT EXACTLY 9:00 P.M. TONIGHT. NOBODY WITHIN THREE BLOCKS. WHEN WE HAVE THE MONEY YOU WILL BE CONTACTED AS TO PICKUP.'

He shook his head. 'These guys have been watching too many crime shows.'

Rybus remained grim. 'You know where this is, right?'

'Sure. They think they're being slick. The park closes at sunset and there are no businesses or residences on that stretch of Lake Drive. It's deserted; there's no reason for anybody to be around. They think they'll pick up the money and split and they'll see if they're being followed. It's easy to get on the freeway from there and head in either direction, or just to get lost in the neighborhoods nearby. Wait a minute.' Theo pulled out his own phone and opened a map, moving his finger around on the screen thoughtfully for a long time.

'It's like I figured. Lake Drive runs north and south around the east side of the park, and connects up with a lot of empty side roads that turn back into city streets after a couple more blocks. There are freeway ramps at both ends of Lake. But here's the thing. They either have to go back out Barlow or else pass one of these two intersections, Adams or Crenshaw at Lake. That means we can stake out three locations and they have to go by one of them.'

'Most important is to get Vanessa back safe. But then, I want them. You're going to have to find out who they are and where they are.'

Theo nodded. 'Understood.'

'Money's ready to go?'

'All set. I'm going to make the pickups now and put it together.'

'I don't want anything to happen until Vanessa is safe. You drop off the money like they say. But then . . . they're mine.'

* * *

The waitress's name was Marla and she was no stranger to dangerous-looking types, but the unfamiliar characters that

32

had jammed together around the table in the back of the coffee shop looked like particular trouble to her. They weren't interested in small talk or niceties and seemed to want her to stay away as much as possible, which was fine by her. She instinctively knew that the less she saw, heard or knew of this crew, the better off she would be.

At the moment they were the only customers in the urban greasy spoon: nine large, serious men with hard expressions, saying little, mostly listening to their obvious leader's hushed words. Only a few had even bothered to order anything, mostly coffee or a soda. The biggest guy, with cornrows and a fedora, ordered a piece of apple pie. Marla made a point of dropping items on the table quickly and moving off without making eye contact of any kind. When she came within ten feet of the table, the conversation ceased and did not resume until she was out of range again.

They weren't threatening her, she decided. They just made it clear they were to be left alone. She was fine with that.

Theo went over the assignments quickly, making sure that everyone understood the roles they had already covered earlier. There would be three vehicles, all black SUVs — two Land Rovers and Theo's own Lincoln Navigator — each carrying three of the crew. The streets that dead-ended onto Lake Drive were in alphabetical order: Ammons, Barlow, Carter. Theo was willing to take one risk (which he hadn't mentioned to Yancey) and have a covert presence within the three-block area mentioned in the text. Two of the cars would be hidden off the road in the dark foliage on Ammons and on Carter, a half block from their intersection with Lake. Theo would make the drop and return up Barlow, where he would wait, similarly concealed, a block from Lake. Anyone coming to pick up the package, from any direction, would have to then pass one of those points. Likely it would be the only car driving through that deserted area. Whoever spotted a vehicle would alert the others by cell phone, wait a short length of time, and follow the car at a distance. The others would be co-ordinated along parallel routes, everybody staying in constant touch with one another, switching off as tail car among them to help allay any suspicion, hopefully following it all the way back to its home base. Theo had already made a dry run through the area to be sure there was cell coverage and there were no dead spots. Losing communication would be disastrous.

Finally Theo looked around the table at them all, staring back at him seriously.

'Any questions? All right then. We got an hour. Let's get to our stations.'

Theo motioned to Marla for the check, which she quickly brought over. She was surprised to see him smile brightly at her as he took it, and she found herself returning the smile shyly before stepping back. She looked long enough to note that his eyes seemed two different colors. The entire crew rose with a scrape of chairs and followed their leader to the register where he settled their insubstantial bill. Felix, the large man who had ordered the pie, reached into his pocket and pulled out a small roll of bills, leaving several on the table for Marla. As they filed out, he nodded to her with an unsettling cockeyed smile.

'Y'all work hard for the money,' he rasped.

Marla didn't feel totally comfortable again until they had been gone a good ten minutes and she was sure they weren't coming back.

* * *

Lake Drive where Barlow Street dead-ended was a dark, wooded intersection without a street light. Theo reflected that it was a good place for a drop like this. He stood in front of the wooden park bench and looked in all directions, sweeping his flashlight around. A few feet behind the bench, plunging into darkness, there was a sudden drop down to the lake. He could see reflections on the water from the lights on the far side, but that was the only ambient light. This was a desolate place at night.

His own SUV was the only car parked

in any direction as far as he could see, and there didn't seem to be anybody in the park itself. The lake was long and narrow, stretching north and south for several blocks. He knew that there were pathways around it, though all was obscured by thick shrubs covering the hill leading down to the lakeside. He doubted anybody would be walking up from the lake.

That meant, as he figured, the only access to this bench had to be along Lake Drive. Anybody coming for the money had to come up or down this road. So far, so good.

Since leaving his Navigator, he had never loosened his tight grip on the knotted black plastic bag in his left hand. A million dollars in stacks of hundreds makes a surprisingly compact package. It's too much to fit into a standard plastic grocery bag — such a bag would start to split before two-thirds of the bills were stuffed tightly into it — but it fits quite loosely into a 45 gallon trash-and-garden bag. He did one final sweep of the area with his light, then turned it off, bent down and shoved the bag under the bench. It killed him to be leaving so much money in the middle of nowhere like this. It was madness. It put so much at risk for the entire organization.

He had to make sure they got it back.

He knew it wasn't her fault, but he still cursed Vanessa for putting them all in this position. And then he cursed Yancey for the astonishing weakness he had revealed. When this was all over, there would need to be some serious re-evaluation of the boss, and maybe some confidential conversations with some of his associates.

He looked at his watch: 9:00. All right then. He stood up and returned to his car. There was not a word in the car from any of the three of them as he got behind the wheel, started up the engine and turned on the headlights. He slowly pulled out from the curb and cruised up Barlow to their stakeout point, a vacant lot full of untrimmed vegetation. His car's big tires had no problem negotiating the curb and pulling in behind a shock of bushes. He killed the lights and they sat back to wait.

Near the intersection of Ammons Street and Lake Drive, one of the Land Rovers sat off the road in a dark gravel turnaround. At 9:22, the occupants noted the approach of a car from further north on Lake. A call went through to Theo.

'Car comin' down Lake. No lights. Passing us now, going slow. Some kinda old Toyota. Looks like just a driver, unless someone else is hunched down in the seats. Not paying us any attention; don't think he made us.'

'Let the other car know too. Everybody stay sharp.'

It was 9:27 when Theo got the next call from Felix in the third vehicle, parked ten feet in from the curb on a stretch of gravel near Carter and Lake.

'Car comin' down Lake away from the drop-off place, with its lights off.'

'You know what to do. Wait 'til he's safely past, then follow. Don't get made. Tell the other car quick.'

Felix was making that call when the dark Toyota passed them, starting to pick up speed down Lake. It lights came on about a third of a block away. His

39

driver gunned the Land Rover's engine to life. Wheels spun, throwing gravel into the air, and with a screech, the SUV bounded forward over the curb onto Carter Street. He took a sharp left onto Lake without slowing and floored the accelerator. His eyes were acclimated to the dark and he would go as far as he could before he risked turning on his headlights. Nate, the young man in the passenger seat, reflexively held his breath. Felix, jammed into the back seat, was frantically speaking into his phone, informing Theo of what was happening.

'He's hanging a left up ahead,' the driver snarled. He waited for the car to disappear up the street and hit his lights. Nate finally exhaled.

Felix breathlessly kept Theo informed of the events as they rapidly unfolded. The Toyota wound its way up and down a few blocks before reaching a major thoroughfare, Third Street, and entering traffic.

Theo's Navigator remained parked by the curb.

'What's up?' came a voice from the back seat.

'Just want to check something out.' He pulled a U-turn on the deserted street and headed back towards Lake Drive. He tossed the phone back. 'Tell them to keep in constant touch.'

'Felix says they pulled into a parking lot. Some kinda market.'

Pulled into a market? Carrying a million in cash? His misgivings were growing stronger now. He had considered a possible diversion; that was why he now was returning to the bench.

'Barry's car has caught up with them. They've both pulled in across the street, where they can keep an eye on the Toyota.'

Theo halted the car just before the intersection and jumped to the pavement, moving quickly towards the bench.

He carefully perused the area. The bag of money was gone. Apparently that was the pickup car after all. Anybody else who had grabbed the money would have had to come from the lake, down there, and that seemed almost impossible.

He looked down over the park. He heard nothing. It was too dark to see anything.

He ran back to the Navigator. In moments they were tearing down the road to join the others at the market.

Across the street from the market, in a darkened trough between two ineffective streetlights, the two dark Land Rovers sat at the curb. Six pairs of eyes were fixed on the beat-up brown Toyota parked askew in its spot in the lot.

Barry had left his car and was standing at the open window of the other vehicle. Nate spoke animatedly to him. 'There was one guy. I saw him getting out of the car as we drove by. He went into the market. Didn't look right or left.'

'What'd he look like?'

'Tall guy. Maybe white, maybe not. All in dark colors, maybe black shirt and pants. Looks like he had a hat pulled over his head. One of those knit caps . . . I think.'

Barry looked at his watch. 'Been a few minutes now. I'm gonna go check inside.'

'Is that a good idea? What if the guy

42

sees you and makes you?'

'What if he went out the back door?'

Nate and Felix exchanged glances.

'He wasn't carrying no bag or nothing,' said Nate. 'If he went out the back, he left the money in the car, right?'

Barry nodded thoughtfully. 'I'm still gonna check this out. You all be ready to roll if he comes out.' He looked up and down the street and, catching a gap in traffic both ways, trotted across to the market.

He was back out only a short time later, running back to the SUVs.

'Nobody in there that looks anything like that,' he panted. 'You sure that's what he looked like?'

'Yeah, I'm sure!'

'You sure he wasn't carrying a bag?'

'Uh . . . pretty sure,' said Nate hesitantly.

Barry sighed. 'We need to go check out the car. I'm gonna give T.C. a call.'

'No need. Here he comes.' Felix jerked his thumb up the street at an approaching set of lights. The Navigator pulled into a parking spot halfway up the block and soon Theo was walking briskly back down the sidewalk towards them. They quickly filled him in on the situation and he stood in exasperated thought for a short time.

'All right. Felix, you come with me into the store. Barry, you think you can pop that Toyota quietly and not draw attention?'

'No problem.'

'Okay, give us about five minutes, and if nobody comes out, go check it out. The rest of you, stay in the cars, someone behind the wheel, and keep an eye out. Call me if anything doesn't look right.' He sighed. 'I'm hoping I'm wrong, but maybe we just got taken.'

The Stop'n'Shop was a small food market with Asian specialties piled into shelves in crowded aisles. There were only two customers, an elderly lady and a younger woman. Both turned with alarm at the sight of the two large fearsome-looking young men with serious expressions; Theo and Felix paid them no mind as they scanned the aisles. The only other person in the market was a bored and tired-looking middle-aged man leaning on the checkout counter.

Theo nudged his chin at a doorway leading to the back. Felix nodded and proceeded toward it. Theo headed for the man behind the counter.

The guy didn't seem scared, or even interested. He droned, 'Can I help ya?'

Theo smiled. 'Looking for a friend I thought came in here a few minutes ago. Tall guy, in black, wearing a knit beanie?'

'Somebody just came through. I didn't really get a look at him. He headed right for the restroom in the back. Happens a lot. People come through, just want to use the restroom. He got a surprise; I keep it locked.'

'So he came back out again, asked you for the key?'

The proprietor shook his head. 'Don't think he came out again. I hope he's not using my storeroom. That's happened a coupla times.' He didn't seem sufficiently concerned by the prospect to investigate.

'Tell me, is there another way out back there?'

'Of course there is. There's a back door

to the alley. That's how we get deliveries.'

Felix came bursting out of the back, shaking his head.

'Nobody back there. Back door's open.'

Theo waited for the big man to join him, then turned back to the grocer. 'And you got no idea what this guy looked like, maybe if he was carrying something?'

The guy shook his head. 'Sorry.'

'So maybe you've got, like security cameras, like that kinda thing, around here? Maybe my friend got captured on video? It's really important that I see if it's him, you know?'

'We got two cameras. One's not working real well right now. That's the one in the back.'

'Well, you think I could get a look at the footage on the other one, the one that might be working?'

'What, right now?'

Theo continued to smile but there wasn't much friendliness left in it. 'Yeah, like, now. Think I could do that?'

'Look, I'm working. I can't just stop and check the video. And I can't just do that for anyone anyway.'

'Doesn't look real busy right now. My friend here can watch the counter for you.'

'Come on, give me a break. I'm the only one here tonight.'

Theo looked around, noting that both ladies had elected to depart from the store in a hurry, then looked back at the counterman. 'That's right. You're the only one here. Except for me and my friend.'

Felix reached across the counter and grasped the man's upper arm, his huge fist closing around it as if it were a straw. Neither of them ever stopped smiling at the guy, but his eyes grew big with alarm.

'Now, how about we go take a look at that footage, what do you say?'

When the two men left the store, Barry was waiting for them just outside the door. He cast a nervous eye around just to be sure nobody saw him holding his automotive lockout tools nonchalantly at his side. Luckily the neighborhood was a rundown and quiet one, with no cops in sight and locals that minded their own business.

'Nothin' in the car. I even popped the

trunk. It's empty. Looks like it was lifted.' He handed a slip of paper to Theo. 'Registration in the glove box.'

Theo took the paper, scanned it, and stuck it into his pocket. Felix was probably right; odds were it was a stolen car. The owner likely would turn out to have nothing to do with any of this. But he'd look into it.

'So the guy's gone?' Barry asked.

'He went out the back, to the alley. Probably had another car stashed on the next block. The security cam in the store was almost useless. There was a second or two of the guy running past. Just his head, his hat and some red hair.' Theo held up a disc. 'Had him make me this, just in case it might turn out useful.'

'He musta had the bag with him. Where else would it be? It's not in the Toyota.'

Theo cursed under his breath. Could luck have gone any worse?

The guy was probably long gone but he gave word for his crew to start scouring the alley and the streets behind the store.

He hoped against hope there would be *something*. There had to be.

★   ★   ★

'What do you mean, the money wasn't there?'

'It wasn't there! I looked! I did it just like we planned. There was a big dark Navigator that drove up Barlow and then turned around and left. I waited a half hour, checked it was clear, and drove down past Ammons to the bench, and there was *nothing*! They're messing with us!'

Lydia's face had grown progressively darker since Brick had come through the door, out of breath, and started stammering out the story.

'Maybe it wasn't them? Maybe you jumped the gun on them?'

'It was exactly the kind of car you said they'd be driving, one of those big black SUVs! I'm telling you, it was them! The whole thing was a setup. They had another car waiting to tail me. They followed me down Lake Drive past

Carter. They thought they were being sly but I made them. There might have been more of them as well. Luckily I made the car switch as I planned.'

'You're sure they didn't follow you after that?'

'No way. I drove around for a while, keeping an eye out for tails. I gave it a good forty minutes before I felt safe to come home. Nobody was on me.'

Lydia stubbed out the cigarette she had just nervously lit. She paced back and forth in the small living room, her arms crossed, scratching her inked forearms.

'So what do we do?' Brick stammered.

'Let me think,' she replied. 'We need to calm down and think this out. Maybe he's still planning to pay us. He wouldn't do anything to endanger Vanessa. He wouldn't.'

'Lydia, he is not going to pay us!' He grabbed her by the shoulders and stared at her. 'Maybe he couldn't get it together in time. Maybe he just decided not to give us the money. Whatever, his plan tonight wasn't to leave us the money, it was to catch me. He's coming after us. We've got to get away before he figures out a way to find us.'

'He's got the money. I know he does.'

'He didn't ask for more time, did he? He texted he'd drop the money. The money's not there. It was a trap!'

'Damn,' she said, pulling away from Brick. 'We need to think this through. We can't panic.' She paced some more. 'Can't panic. Can't.'

'I know you were sure he'd pay, but it's looking like you were wrong. We've got to cut our losses and run. Tonight.'

'Cut our losses? What does that mean? I'm not going to hurt that sweet girl! We have to keep her safe!'

'I wouldn't do anything to hurt her either. If we have to let her go, we'll let her go.'

'I will not just abandon her somewhere at night in the city. We'll drop her off tomorrow as we planned, no matter what happens. Maybe we can try communicating with him one more time, this time really tough. He doesn't know we won't hurt her. Are you absolutely sure there's no way he can trace us through the phone?'

'Absolutely positive. But I say no more communication. Anything we say to him might tip our hand somehow.' It was suddenly becoming clear to Brick just how scared he was of Yancey Rybus and his associates, and just how bad an idea this whole thing had been, no matter how appealing Lydia's arguments might have seemed.

That was the moment that the phone on the table began to buzz. They both turned and stared at it for a long interval. Finally Lydia broke the spell and went to pick it up. She silently stared at the screen.

'What? What's he say?' Brick asked.

She held the screen up for him to read the message screaming back at them. They looked at each other in stunned bewilderment.

U GOT UR MONEY. NOW GIVE ME BACK MY VANESSA.

3

When Webster Musgrave started his day, he had no expectation of becoming a very rich man, nor of complicating his life in ways previously unimagined.

Webster thoroughly enjoyed his job at the city's Department of Parks, Recreation and Waterfront. He loved being outdoors, in some of the best parts of the city, where there were still trees, fields, flowers, and wildlife. He felt he was doing his part to protect the birds and animals he so loved, and to preserve the little bit of pristine open land remaining in the midst of urban sprawl.

In fact, all of these were factors as to why that morning he was asked to step into his supervisor's office to be summarily fired.

'Web, we had another complaint about you hassling visitors at the Aquatic Park. You've been warned numerous times.' His field manager, Karlotta, had a 'had it up to here' expression on her face that told him this time was the last.

He had to try to argue his case anyway. 'Karly, the kid picked up one of the turtles in the pond and was carrying him around. He almost dropped him a couple times on the rocks! The parents did nothing to stop him. In fact, they were laughing and taking pictures of the little monster! I had to say something!'

'Yes you did. But to call the kid a 'spawn of Satan'?' And the parents say you called them a few choice names as well, and said they weren't fit to raise slugs? Really?'

'Sure, I got a little hot under the collar and said a few unfortunate things . . . '

'*Unfortunate* is putting it mildly! And they said you actually physically handled the kid!'

'Well, I took the turtle away from him. I mean, I had to do that, right?'

'They say you pushed the kid into the lake!'

'That's not how I'd describe it. He slipped on the rocks and fell in.'

Karlotta sighed deeply. 'Webster, this

isn't the first time we've gotten complaints about you. There was that woman with the trash bags.'

'She was just dumping her trash in the park! I couldn't let that go!'

'You dumped the bag's contents all over the woman!'

'That was an accident! I thought the bag was tied up!'

'Web, I'm sorry. I've got no choice but to let you go.' She looked sadly at him. 'I hate to do this. We all love you around here, but you're just causing too much trouble, and the city is giving me a lot of grief because of it.' She held up a hand when she saw he was about to start up again. 'It's a done deal. Look, I'll do what I can to get you severance pay through next week, and I'm not going to embarrass you by having security escort you out or anything. But you have to go, right now. Please!'

Webster hung his head and slumped his shoulders, at a loss for anything to say in his defense. He knew it wouldn't do any good anyway.

Karlotta stood up, sadly walked around

her desk, and actually gave him a hug. 'Good luck.'

Shortly thereafter, Webster Musgrave found himself dazedly stumbling through the DPRW building, carrying a small cardboard box with the few personal items he had had kept in his locker, trying to make sense of what had just happened.

By the time he reached his car in the parking lot, it had occurred to him he had a longer list of problems than he originally realized. He had just lost a job he loved, but there was also Evangeline, his girlfriend. She had been bugging him to apply for one of the upcoming promotions in the department. Their plans to 'get serious' and secure a secure future together were jeopardized unless one or both of them could come up with a larger income. She clearly was not happy with her current job and hoped to quit . . . if he could support them. It had gotten to be a major issue between them.

Web had balked at the idea of applying for an office job with greater authority and pay because it would take him out of the field, where he loved working. They put the topic on hold while Evangeline took two weeks' vacation to visit her folks in Buffalo. He had decided he'd apply for the job despite his misgivings. He'd still be connected to the parks and would find some way to spend time in them with the waterfowl and the turtles. He had been looking forward to pleasantly surprising her upon her return, and to that end hadn't been all that communicative with her since she had left. Now he dreaded that return and the not-so-pleasant surprise that would be awaiting her. Suddenly he felt an overwhelming, crushing sense of impending doom.

He sat in his car for a long time, staring dazedly out the windshield at the stores across the street from the parking lot. He didn't want to go home. He didn't know where he wanted to go. Right this minute, he wished he could be nowhere.

His gaze idly swept over a pet store, a coffee shop, Sundown Liquors . . .

Web was not a drinker by any means, but suddenly it seemed a great idea to pick up something powerfully alcoholic and just go somewhere and drink it. He checked the contents of his wallet.

At this point, Webster considered, he should probably start being frugal with his money, considering there wouldn't be much of it coming in for the foreseeable future. On the other hand, spending a few bucks wasn't going to make much of a difference now. He was out of his car and across the street in a flash.

He had been in this store a number of times, but always to buy soda or a candy bar. Being unfamiliar with liquor, it took him a while to figure out what he should buy, but he decided something that was sweet and fruity might appeal to him. He liked peach soda so he settled on a pint of peach brandy, the cheapest one, carrying the store's own label. It was a hundred proof, whatever that meant. Leaving with his brown-bagged purchase, he wondered where he could go to sip it and think about what he should do next.

The Aquatic Park was walking distance away, easily accessible from the DPRW center, and he was already feeling as if he would be missing it terribly. It was peaceful and familiar. He had a lovely warm day to sit in the sun and just commune with the trees, the grass and the birds, and make his goodbyes to all of them. Besides, if he was going to be drinking, he shouldn't be driving. He was sure nobody would notice, much less mind, if he left his car there in the lot for a few more hours.

With his brown paper package in hand, he headed off towards the south entrance to the Aquatic Park.

It was a gorgeous, perfect day. The sun was hot, the grass was cool and soft, and the scents and sounds of a favorite place filled his senses. He strolled around the lake, happily taking it all in: the lizards and turtles sunning themselves, the ducks and egrets on the lake, even the crows and gulls loudly proclaiming their presence. The only thing he didn't want to be around was people: obnoxious kids abusing the animals, obnoxious adults scattering their litter. He walked until he found a deserted stretch of narrow pathway where he could lie out beneath a tree, surrounded by shrubs. It was very comfortable. Behind him was a very steep hill densely covered with bushes; nobody would be coming down from that direction to disturb him. He unscrewed the brandy bottle and took an experimental sip. It was heady and strong, but very tasty!

Before long, the lovely day, the lovely setting, and a few more sips of the lovely brandy combined to start to dispel his malaise.

Web didn't feel much like thinking out his problems just at this moment. There was time. He was just beginning to feel rather happy again. He took a swallow of the brandy, smelled the roses and lilacs around him, and actually smiled. He pulled out his cellphone and turned it off. Nobody would be calling him except a telemarketer and he didn't want to interrupt the one happy reverie of the day.

Time became a very flexible object; was this something that alcohol did? It seemed quite wonderful and hilariously funny as he realized the sun was actually low in the sky, the shadows were deepening and it was beginning to get a little chilly, and he could have sworn he had just gotten there!

He took a swig from the brandy bottle and saw it was almost empty. That seemed funny to him and he started to quake with quiet laughter. Was he drunk? He couldn't be sure. But he definitely was sleepy. And things were sort of swirling around in odd ways. He laid back against his dear friend the tree and closed his eyes. Just for a moment.

He didn't exactly wake up; it was more like his consciousness reluctantly decided to return. His mouth was dry, his head ached, and he felt chilly. His neck was stiff and his back hurt from the hard bark of the tree that had been supporting him.

Obviously the park had closed some time ago. It was quiet and dark. The only light came from the street far past the park, reflecting over the intervening lake. What time was it? He looked at his wristwatch, turning his wrist in various directions to try to pick up some of the slim reflected light. With his bleary vision, he couldn't be sure, but he thought it said 9:00. Could that be? Had he been out here all this time?

He picked up the empty brandy bottle lying alongside him, feeling confused and, he decided, rather ashamed of himself. He had gotten himself drunk and had passed out, for an unbelievably long time. He was feeling like a failure again, and now like a degenerate as well. Good thing the park was closed and nobody was here; the last thing he wanted was for someone to see him here and expect him to explain himself.

He heard the low throb of a large car engine coming from not too far away. The car seemed to stop very close by, and the engine was shut off. Then footsteps, directly behind and above him: shuffling through leaves and gravel. Webster froze in place, holding his breath, not daring to move or even exhale.

Someone, about eight feet overhead, was walking along the rim of the park. It sounded as if they dropped something, and then pushed it along the ground. Some loose dirt rolled down the hill towards him through the thick bushes. Then the footsteps resumed, moving away. There were the sounds of a car door opening and closing, the engine starting up again, and its gradual fading off as the car drove away. After a good ten minutes of silence, he decided to chance a peek, to see if they (whoever *they* were) had disappeared.

His eyes had become accustomed to the dark and he was able to pick out openings between the bushes sufficiently to slowly squeeze his way up the embankment. When his eyes were level with the top of the hill, he stuck his head out and looked back and forth.

He was directly behind a bench of some kind and should have been able to see between the legs underneath the seat, but something had been stuck in there that obstructed his view. He reached out and touched it; it was a plastic trash bag.

Another one of those people leaving their trash, spoiling the park. Web couldn't help it. He no longer worked for the department, and it was no longer his job to look after such things, but he still saw it as his greater duty. He pulled the bag towards him. There had to be a trash can nearby. Why were people such pigs, they couldn't just find a trash can?

Deciding he was alone, he was about to scramble up next to the bench, when he heard a car approaching. There were no lights, but he could hear it coming. It was an older car that needed a tune-up.

He was still terrified of the idea of being found out here; the mortification would be too much for him to take. He pulled the bag out and allowed himself to slide back down the hill quickly, pulling the bag along under the scrub. When he reached the tree, he curled up and once again froze and held his breath.

The new car stopped close by but the engine kept running. A car door opened. There were more footprints, more shuffling. Once again he waited for what felt like an hour for the sound of the footprints to subside, the slam of the car door, and the sound of the sputtering engine as the car drove away.

What was going on up there tonight? Did they leave more trash? Would there be more people coming? Web didn't want to find out; he just wanted to get away.

He continued to sit motionless, silent. The moment he felt it was safe, he would get up and . . .

The sound of still another car, another large one, approaching. Web flattened himself against the tree and tried to make himself as silent and still as possible.

More footsteps, more shuffling and crunching, then an agonizingly long interval while the person seemed to stand still only eight feet above Webster. Did they know he was there? Finally they turned and walked away; there were the slamming of the car door, a sudden roar as the engine accelerated, and a squeal of tires. The vehicle's noises faded away into the night above him.

That was enough for Webster. He decided to get out while he could. As soon as it seemed sufficiently quiet to be safe, he stood up, hoisted the bag over his shoulder, and hustled off as fast as he dared down the dark lakeside path toward where he had entered the park.

Luckily he knew his way quite well around the lake, and soon he reached its south end. He knew exactly where he'd find a trash can and headed for it.

The bag felt as if it weighed maybe twenty pounds or so, filled about three-quarters up with what felt like paper batches of some kind. When he reached the trash can, he stopped just before dumping the bag. His curiosity got the better of him; he struggled with the tight knots that had been tied in the top of the bag until he got them open, and peered inside.

If he had any doubts whether or not he was sober again, he knew he was now.

He stared down into a bag full of packets of bills. A bag of money. A *lot* of money.

Webster looked around until he was sure nobody else was in the park. He knotted up the bag and lit off for his car. He knew he'd have no trouble getting it out of the department parking lot; he had worked late many times. He also knew it was not likely he'd run into anyone there at this time of night. In short order, he was driving home, the bag of money on the floor of the passenger seat beside him.

4

One of the more tedious duties of a police detective arises when he or she is called upon to testify in court regarding an investigation and arrest. Tuesday morning was such a time for Detective Marlon Morrison. He had been impatiently sitting in a courtroom in the Criminal Courts Building since it had opened and had finally been called to give testimony just before the judge called lunch recess. At least, he considered, he wouldn't have to come back after lunch. He could bid the Criminal Courts farewell for the day, and grab a meatball hero at his favorite deli on the way back to the station.

His time on the stand had been fairly short: a few questions from the Assistant District Attorney and then some rapid cross-examination from the defense attorney. He thought he had acquitted himself well under cross-examination, but the dagger looks he got from the ADA (and the smug smile from the defense table as he was dismissed from the stand) made him think the only *acquittal* she saw in the cards was for the accused. Well, he had done the best he could. It was a robbery-assault case and he had caught the guy with the stolen property in his possession. So what if he had overlooked a few of the niceties about the arrest and just maybe skipped a step or two in the paperwork he prepared? It looked open and shut to him: the guy was guilty as pure sin. He still didn't understand all the hoops he and his fellow detectives were expected to jump through. He missed the old days when things were so much simpler.

At least, he reflected as he finally headed back to work, some things hadn't changed. The deli's meatball hero was still tasty. He still had a satisfied smile on his face as the elevator door opened to his squad room.

He recalled that when he first came on board, the unit had officially been called Special Crimes; going even further back, it had gone by the prosaic but accurate title Robbery-Homicide. At some point, the department had decided Personal Crimes bore more solemnity. The unit still dealt with basically the same types of felonies: homicides, severe assaults, robberies. Simultaneously, the unit that handled burglaries and similar nonviolent crimes, currently housed in a similar squad room one flight up from them, had gained the moniker Property Crimes. To Marlon's way of thinking, there had been little difference in their function beyond the name changes. It was just window dressing.

Marlon had just deposited himself before his computer and stacks of files when he looked up to see his lieutenant, Hank Castillo, standing over the desk, holding out a yellow phone slip.

'Morrison, I believe you're up. The call just came in. DB up in the hills.'

'Aw, Lou, I'm swamped here. Nobody else can handle it?'

'Right now, you're the man.' Castillo dropped the slip on the desk in front of Marlon. 'Better get up there. They tell me it's a ripe one.' Without further ceremony, he turned to head back to his office.

Marlon picked up the slip and sighed. An address way up in the hills. Just what he needed. He rose from his chair and trudged back to the elevator.

As he drove to the crime scene, he reflected how he felt he sometimes got a bad rap in Personal Crimes as a slacker. He didn't consider himself a bad cop; he was smart and, in his own way, he cared. He had a lot of experience as a detective with the unit and had cleared his share of cases. The thing was, he was less than two years from retirement at this point, and he just wanted to ride it out, get his pension, and find a peaceful spot to spend the rest of his life. That was it, he decided: he simply wanted some peace and quiet. He had a long history of hard work, frustration, violent confrontation, and daily encounters with lowlife. He was tired of being on the firing line. All he wanted was to get away from the criminals and the slime-bags and to be left alone. Was that so bad? He'd seen too many of his colleagues burn out or get seriously hurt, even killed. It was no longer worth that to him, not when the end was so close.

He'd had a few partners who, for one reason or another, had terminated their relationship. One transferred out of Personal Crimes into Narcotics; one left the department entirely. He'd been a solo for a while now, and he silently hoped it would stay that way. There was an advantage in having a partner to shoulder part of the work, but as he saw it, that was outweighed by the disadvantages. Partners tended to generate more work and more effort to begin with.

Marlon had other former partners as well: two ex-wives, to one of whom he was still making alimony payments. He had no interest in finding a new partner of that type either at the moment. Getting involved, no matter in what way, was just too much work and he was just too tired.

★ ★ ★

The quiet winding road up toward the state park at the top of the hills was called Blaisdell Drive, the site of older homes nestled back from the road behind trees and manicured lawns. Marlon saw the flashing lights and the numerous vehicles parked at one bend of the road and pulled over.

There were already vans from the Scientific Investigation Division and the county Coroner's Office and just beyond the parked vehicles, an area had been taped off with skeins of bright yellow police tape. A beat-up open-bed pickup truck seemed to be the focus of attention of the various personnel on the scene. Marlon flashed his badge and one of the patrol officers let him through the tape into the action.

'Vizcaino's one of the guys who made the stop,' the officer said, waving to another uniform who came over to join them as they walked towards the truck. He now could see there was a very old model white refrigerator lying on its side behind the pickup. A length of chain with an attached padlock lay alongside as well as a large pair of bolt cutters that had been used to break open the chain. Two techs in blue SID coveralls, and a young woman with a vinyl windbreaker that read CORONER across the back, were standing nearby, apparently awaiting Marlon's arrival.

'So where'd this come from?' Marlon asked, noting that there was already a ripe stink in the air. He had never gotten used to the smell of dead bodies.

Vizcaino had a deep voice to go with his large size. 'Do you know the big open area just before you get to the park up at the top of the hill, just inside of city limits? You'd be amazed at the kind of junk people dump there: appliances, stoves, desks, even sofas. This was a body dump. The victim was deposited inside that refrigerator and it was closed up with that chain and padlock.'

'So how'd he end up down here?' Marlon cursed his luck again. The makeshift dump area was almost out of the city limits. This could have been a case for another jurisdiction and some other detective.

'Apparently the guy with the truck drives various neighborhoods to see if anything of value's been dumped. He and his pal came by and found the fridge this morning, so they loaded it onto the bed, and as they came down the hill, it started to fall off the bed of the truck. The door popped partly open against the chain. My partner and I happened to be parked along the road here . . . '

Marlon nodded. He didn't say the first thing that occurred to him: they were goofing off in a remote untraveled part of town. His cynicism never stopped growing. He really needed to get to retirement.

' . . . We saw the fridge bouncing around ready to tumble off the truck, and pulled him over. We got one whiff of it and, well, here we all are.' Vizcaino pointed across the crime scene area to where his partner stood with two unhappy-looking guys in soiled clothing. 'We've got 'em when you want to talk to 'em.'

Marlon thanked the officer, who left to join his partner and the unlucky scavengers. The medical examiner approached him and put out her hand, which he did not take.

'They told us you were coming,' she said, 'so we held up until you could get a look at everything before we started processing. I'm Sela Hovsepian from the ME's office.' She looked to be in her late twenties. Marlon wasn't happy about that; a green young assistant would mean more work on his part to follow up on information. He didn't necessarily like it that much better when one of the real pros, like the veteran Mickey Kendrick, were on the case because then they'd get through the process *too* fast and he'd be expected to keep up. In Marlon's experience, a dead body had not yet stood up and walked away. A DB was a DB and would keep as his investigation proceeded with due speed. He liked the MEs in the middle, who knew their stuff but kept things on an even keel.

By now the smell was really getting pungent. Marlon nodded to her and pulled a handkerchief out of his pocket and held it over his nose.

'So are you ready for the grand opening?' she said brightly.

'Oh, lord,' muttered Marlon. Without

further ado, she yanked on the refrigerator door, which separated and fell onto the ground. The victim was stuffed inside the space, wrapped in a large sheet of translucent plastic and folded in a way that didn't look physically possible.

She was stronger than she looked; she skillfully slid the body out of the space and onto the pavement next to the refrigerator. She took a pair of shears out of a bag lying on the ground beside her and gently began to cut away the plastic, peeling it back, until the body began to reveal itself. The odor did not seem to bother her in the least. Marlon, several steps away and uncomfortable, couldn't understand it.

It was a young man in a white T-shirt and undershorts. Marlon saw the swirl of bright blue stars that had recently been tattooed up and down one side of his neck as the young ME unwrapped the body. It was clearly stiff: she carefully, gradually inspected it with some difficulty, looking closely at the limbs and extremities.

'How long do you think he's been

dead?' Marlon asked through the ker-chief. 'It must have been a long time to smell that bad.'

'Not really. I'll tell better with further examination, but I'm thinking he was only in there maybe a day.'

'What?'

'There's still rigidity. As you likely know, rigor mortis begins to set in after a couple of hours and begins to go away after twenty-four to thirty-six hours.'

'Uh, of course. But the smell . . . '

'Well, yesterday was a warm day and today's been the same. The victim was sealed up inside a box that holds heat. Bodies can start smelling pretty quickly under the right conditions. But he doesn't really smell all that bad to me.' She reached into her bag. 'I'll be better able to tell when I take the liver temp.' She looked up at Marlon. 'Care to inspect the body before I get to work?'

With a sigh of resignation, Marlon squatted down next to the ME, pocketed his kerchief, and pulled out a pair of plastic gloves that all the detectives carried for such situations. He held his breath as long as he could. No clothing, so no wallet, no identification. No wristwatch, no jewelry articles of any kind.

'Whoever killed him did a thorough job of stripping the body,' Marlon muttered, trying not to exhale too much. 'I don't think there's anything to be found that would be of any help.'

'This would be the actual cause of death,' she said, turning the victim's head over and pointing to the entry wound in the temple. 'One shot at close range. This was an execution.'

After all his years as a policeman, this was still something he couldn't get used to. It was a big reason he was ready and eager to finish up his time and leave the force. Part of him just wanted to leave it all behind right now.

Part of him, however, suddenly wanted to find the lowlife who could do something like this.

Marlon pulled out his phone and snapped some photos of the deceased, then stood up, looking over at the two waiting SID techs and then back at the young ME. He allowed himself to breathe. 'I guess I can leave him to all of you now. Let me know what you find.'

A cursory interview with the guys from the pickup truck was useless. As Vizcaino had speculated, they'd picked up the refrigerator despite its age because it looked to be worth a few bucks as scrap. It apparently hadn't bothered them that it was unusually heavy or was wrapped in a chain. Clearly, he considered, they weren't brain surgeons moonlighting as trash scavengers.

There was nothing more here, he figured. Back to the squad room.

When he returned to the unit, Marlon was surprised to find a familiar balding, stocky figure in a worn-out sports jacket sitting at his desk, chatting with two of the other detectives, Frank Vandegraf and Leon Simpkins. He rose with a smile to greet Marlon.

'Hope you don't mind I swiped your chair, partner.' He extended a hand, which Marlon hesitantly shook.

'Gene. How are things in Narcotics?'

'Meh. The usual.'

'What brings you over here to Personal? Not missing us, are you?'

Gene Hogan and Marlon Morrison had been partners in Personal Crimes some years earlier. They had worked together reasonably well, Marlon felt, but he had never really been comfortable around the guy. He was sure that Gene felt the same and that had been part of the reason he had finally transferred across town to Narcotics. The relationship had never been one that would inspire a visit for old times' sake.

'I had to come over to Property Crimes upstairs to talk to someone. Got a minute for a cup of coffee down in the commissary?'

'Uh . . . yeah. Sure.'

Marlon was not one for small talk. They sat silently, staring over cardboard cups of coffee across the table, while he waited for Hogan to make his point.

'I hear you picked up a DB today.'

'News travels fast. How'd you hear that?'

Hogan shrugged. 'I stuck my head in

the unit to say hi and heard the word. Something about what I heard struck a chord. Body dump in the hills?'

Marlon nodded. 'So?'

'Know anything about the vic? ID, anything?'

'Not yet. Young guy, just a kid. Body was stripped. Why the interest?'

'I might be able to help you. We're following the Rybus organization pretty closely.'

'Of course you are. You think they're connected to this?'

'It's possible. Got a photo, anything, of the vic?'

Marlon pulled out his phone and keyed up one of the photos of the dead man. Hogan examined it carefully, then handed back the phone.

'Star tats on his neck. Not familiar to me. But he might be one of Rybus's soldiers.'

'So are you saying that someone's edging in on Rybus's territory, maybe killing off some of his guys?'

'He's pretty strong just now. He eliminated or absorbed the competition quite efficiently. More likely it's in the family. Rumor is he's got a very efficient enforcer and keeps him busy.'

'That's a lot of theory, Gene. How's that of any help to me?'

Hogan smiled and shrugged genially. 'Give me a couple days. Maybe I can find out more for you. Let me know what else you learn; we might be able to help each other here.'

Marlon judged that to actually mean that he might be able to help Gene. The guy was never exactly the magnanimous sort. He drained the last of his cup and stood up. 'Okay. Good to see you. I better get back to it.'

Hogan also stood up, extending his hand to shake. 'Back into the fray? Where's this newfound enthusiasm coming from, anyway? You're usually looking for the least possible amount of work. Turning into a go-getter in your old age? Anyway, let's keep in touch on this, okay? You know where to find me.'

Marlon shook his hand, resisting the urge to reply that his *newfound enthusiasm* came from wanting to get away from

Gene Hogan. It was pretty clear what was going on here: Gene was spinning his wheels at Narcotics and needed a leg up on something, anything.

It did make sense, he reflected as he returned to his unit. This was a gangster execution . . . why not an in-house killing of some dissident or disloyal member of the organization? Yancey Rybus was infamous, to cops and criminals alike, as a ruthless disciplinarian. It at least afforded Marlon someplace from where to start, and, he realized he actually did have some kind of newfound enthusiasm. For some reason, this one mattered to him.

5

While Marlon was sitting in court Tuesday morning, contemplating the utter futility of the court system, Webster Musgrave was sitting cross-legged on his bedroom floor, contemplating the cause of his sleepless night. After his long nap in the park the previous evening, he hadn't been sleepy to begin with, and his head had been spinning and throbbing all night long. The pain reliever he had taken for his unfamiliar hangover hadn't helped him fall asleep, as he learned later, when he looked at the label and saw it contained a large dose of caffeine.

He surveyed the scene in the small front room of his tiny abode: the front door locked, blinds pulled tightly closed, stacks of money scattered all around him. He had counted it all at least a half dozen times over the night, repeatedly riffling through every bill in every packet.

One hundred stacks of bills, each

containing one hundred bills and wrapped with a band of self-stick paper.

He had one million dollars in hundred-dollar bills. One million. Placed in a knotted plastic trash bag that had been stashed in a closed, deserted city park.

Questions swirled through his pounding mind in a torrent. He had tried to calm down and take them in order.

Where had it come from? To whom did it belong?

Logically, there was something criminal involved in this. Was it stolen? A bank robbery, maybe? Had he unwittingly blundered into the middle of a drug deal? Was it counterfeit money, to be sold at a percentage of its face value and then be passed as real, as in stories he had read?

The next question that arose: should he keep it? Or should he try to return it?

Webster liked to believe he was an honest man, but could trying to return it get him in trouble . . . or even killed? Besides, he considered his own money problems and his relationship problems that came down to money. Wouldn't it be a win-win situation if he kept it, and spent it slowly? If the money was illicit, he'd be stealing from crooks and solving his own worries while protecting his own neck.

But suppose the money were counterfeit? He could get in enormous trouble trying to spend it.

Another thought: in those stories he loved, often the illicit money had been marked by the authorities. Maybe the serial numbers were on record. Maybe they had some special invisible dye or some other sophisticated tag. If he tried to spend any of it, he might end up getting arrested himself!

And still another thought: suppose this was ransom money, for some loved one somewhere? This kind of thing happened in those stories too, a drop-off of a lot of cash at some remote location. What if his holding back the money put an innocent (or even not so innocent) person in jeopardy?

His head still hammered. He couldn't think straight. He'd have to give this a lot more thought, sort out all the possibilities.

One thing he definitely had to do was

find a safe way to store the money away. He couldn't keep it in that bag. Maybe he could rent a safe deposit box . . . no, too small. A commercial storage area? No, too big. Anything public seemed too much of a risk.

He had decided that he was safe enough for the moment. Nobody had seen him take the money. Nobody had followed him. Nobody could link him to it. He could temporarily hide the money and leave the apartment.

The first thing he needed to do was to get some kind of box to stash it in. He checked his watch. Clips, the office supply chain store down the street, would be open. He could drive over and get a box. No, he was in no shape to drive. He could walk.

He scooped up all the packets of bills, piling them in different ways on the floor, then rummaged through a cabinet drawer for a tape measure. He made rough measurements of what size carton would hold it all.

It was amazing how small a space could be occupied by a million dollars. In his imagination, it would have filled a walk-in closet. This would fit in a box not too much bigger than a standard-size office filing box.

He tossed all the packets back into the plastic bag and jammed the bag into his closet. He actually found himself talking reassuringly to the bag: 'I'll lock the door and I'll be right back. You'll be safe in here.' He realized, as he shut the closet door, that he was trying to reassure himself.

He walked out the driveway from his back house and almost got hit by a small green car that braked to a halt as he absent-mindedly crossed the street from between two parked cars. He held out a hand in a 'Sorry' gesture and moved on, realizing he'd better pay a little more attention to his surroundings.

A half hour later, he returned with a three-pack of folded cardboard boxes. It was easy to assemble one, sixteen inches square and about eight inches deep. He pulled out the bag of money and dumped the bills on the ground, then began to fill the box with the stacks. He couldn't get an order that satisfied him, and kept rearranging, removing and replacing. Then he dumped everything back on the floor and started picking through each pile again, struggling to pay attention and think straight.

All at once, he realized he had been kneeling here on the floor, with the piles of money, for hours now. It was early afternoon. His knees ached. He had arranged and rearranged the stacks of bills until he had found the most compact matrix in the 16″ by 16″ cardboard carton. Several of the stacks of bills were laid out on the floor around him.

Evangeline often told him he was borderline OCD, obsessive-compulsive disorder. Possibly she had a point.

He figured he must have once again counted through every single one of the bills, examining everything repeatedly until they were as familiar as old friends. Almost none of the bills were consecutive in number; some were new and crisp, some were older and more worn.

Who would have access to so many hundred-dollar bills and what had to be a machine to stack and band them so neatly? A bank? The mob (was there such a thing anymore, or was it just a figment of television and movies)? Drug dealers? He had already judged the money to not be counterfeit; it certainly looked and felt authentic, and he could even see watermarks in the bills when he held them up to the light. Besides, there was just too much variation in serial numbers and condition. He didn't really know all that much about how counterfeiters worked, but it stood to reason they couldn't create such randomness. He'd read that counterfeiters would run their newly printed bills through a clothes dryer to make them appear wrinkled and used, but he figured there would still be some semblance of uniformity when they were done. Certainly there were lawful individuals and institutions with enough money to put this together, but he couldn't figure a legitimate reason to put so much cash together in neat piles of hundreds and deposit them into a trash bag left on a dark street. No, this was clearly part of an extra-legal deal.

So he had stumbled into the aftermath of a bank robbery, an in-progress underworld deal for drugs or weapons . . . or a ransom payment. But there had been no news on TV or radio about a kidnapping. But of course the person paying the ransom would have been warned not to notify the police, wouldn't they? That was how it was always done in the movies.

The more he thought about it, the less likely it seemed that he was endangering someone's life by having this money. Maybe it was rationalizing, but what could he do about it now, anyway? There was no way he could return this money. He was powerless to help anyone.

And besides, he needed it. The box in front of him held the answers to all his problems.

But could he take the chance to actually spend any of it? Was it marked? It didn't appear to be, but he had no idea what to look for: invisible inks that only showed up under black light or whatever? Were the serial numbers, as random as they were, on record? Were there authorities — or gangsters — out looking for it right now? A million dollars: certainly *someone* was looking for it. Could they trace it to him?

His headache hadn't gone away, but it had subsided to a dull pain. His stomach was likewise feeling a bit more settled. He realized he hadn't eaten all day and he was hungry, but there was almost nothing to eat in the house.

Slapping one of the packets against the palm of his hand, Webster decided to risk spending one of the bills. Hundred-dollar bills were no longer all that unusual. In the right place, they might not even get a second look.

He could go to one of those big-box stores or supermarkets and use it at the self-checkout machine. Then he wouldn't even have to interact with a checkout person. If the bill turned out to be flagged in some way, they might not be able to trace it to him.

But there were security cameras. There were cameras everywhere.

He'd have to wear a hat, pulled down

low, and the most unobtrusive clothes he owned. No trademarks or graphics on the shirt. Nothing to identify him beyond being a male of a certain age range. This could work. He'd spend one bill for food, at that gigantic food market a few blocks away . . . stock provisions so he wouldn't have to leave his home for a few days, then wait and see what happened.

The time was now. He couldn't stay in here fidgeting and fussing any longer. He couldn't sleep. He hadn't eaten, beyond a cup of coffee. He had to get out and take action. Maybe then he could relax and start to think straight.

He slid one bill out of the packet and dropped the rest back in the box, gathering up the wrapped bills around him and carefully stacking them, then folding the flaps of the box together and depositing the carton up on a shelf in his closet.

He found himself talking to the money box again. 'You'll be safe up here. I'll be back soon.' Then he sorted through his dresser, giggling nervously, 'I just haven't a thing to wear, heh heh,' before he caught himself.

'I'm losing it,' he said aloud to himself. 'If I don't get some food and sleep, I'll never think this through clearly.'

He picked his way through the aisles at Food Extravaganza, dropping items into his cart such as frozen pizza, milk, bread, peanut butter, some fruit and vegetables. He avoided contact of any sort with employees or other customers, which wasn't difficult. The customers were all self-involved, often on their cellphones, and the employees seemed to be chiefly interested in avoiding customers. In his dark sweatshirt, jeans, and baseball cap, Webster figured he blended in as a nondescript shopper. The self-check lines were busy and he had to wait in line for an open machine, then he swept each item through the scanner.

Now came the nerve-wracking part. He fished the bill out of his pocket and fed it into the bill slot, holding his breath. He remembered reading in a news article that many of these machines had sophisticated detectors. If his bill was indeed counterfeit, it could be picked up. If it gave off some kind of alarm, he was ready to turn and hustle for the door. He had his direct route picked out.

There was no alarm. The machine simply spit out his change and a receipt and the touch screen screamed THANK YOU in huge letters. Still dazed, he gathered his change, picked up his bags of food and headed out the door. He swiftly strode home, feeling a giddy sense of exhilaration at the danger he had escaped. He wasn't used to this much adrenaline.

When he got to Shafford Avenue, he slowed down, relieved that he wasn't being followed or observed. Shortly he reached the driveway that led to his small back house. The street was clear; there was nobody out front to see him, not even his ubiquitous landlady. He was home free.

6

By the time Marlon was arriving in court Tuesday morning, Theo had already started his day, getting a jump on tracking down Vanessa's captors. Last night's meeting with Rybus had not gone well; the boss never lost his characteristic cool but made clear his extreme displeasure that the abductors were allowed to elude their tail. Theo had no choice but to promise quick results, privately hoping that they would release Vanessa as promised and that he could pick up their trail in the meantime.

The first thing he did was to delegate all of the overseeing of day-to-day collections and distributions to his own lieutenants. His normal business day involved a constant flow of meet-ups and giving of orders, and he'd need to devote his full energies to the matter at hand. Yancey wasn't going to like that either, but Theo had no choice.

He had already put out the word through every channel about a big white dude with curly red hair and a scraggly beard. They had started to refer to him as Big Red. Whoever he was working with, the guy knew something about their organization. Theo increasingly suspected that Big Red and his crew knew him as well. He had few facts to go on but he was pushing them as hard as he could, leaning hard on everyone he could call in, and offering a good reward for the proper information: the carrot and the stick that were the tried-and-true Yancey Rybus method.

He took it upon himself to track down the owner of the stolen Toyota. The car had likely been reported and towed away by now, but he had the registration. It was early enough that he might catch the guy before he went to work.

That morning Theo found himself in front of a row house along San Cristobal Street. He climbed the steps and rang the doorbell. A middle-aged man answered, eyeing Theo warily.

'Sorry to bother you. I'm looking for Luis Molino.'

'That's me. Who are you?'

Theo, affecting an officious attitude, had taken out his wallet and opened and closed it quickly before the man could see anything. 'Do you happen to own a 1997 Toyota Corolla sedan?'

'What, do you know where it is? Did somebody find it?'

'So you do own one, right?'

'It's been missing since Saturday! Stolen from the airport when I went to see my sister off! Where is it?'

'And you reported it stolen?'

'Hell yes, of course I did! Do you have it, or don't you?' He looked Theo up and down. 'You're a cop? You don't look like a cop.'

'Grand Theft Auto unit. Undercover.' Theo, a natural actor and chameleon, instinctively went with the role. 'I believe we've located your vehicle. Do you have a copy of your police report that you can show me, sir?'

Molino was too excited by the prospect of getting his car back to think about asking Theo for any further identification . . . as yet. 'Yeah, sure. Hold on, I'll get it for you. Wait here.' He returned to the door shortly and thrust a sheet of paper at Theo.

'You say it was taken from the airport?' Theo said, pretending to peruse the document carefully, just to avoid further eye contact with the man.

'Yeah! Yeah! From the short-term lot, you know? When I got back, it was just gone, like that. I was only in the terminal with her for maybe twenty minutes! I guess I shouldn't have left the ticket on the dash, huh? I heard they cruise those lots looking for cars to boost, but my old beater? I figured it must have been for the parts. If it ever turned up again, I figured it'd be in pieces.'

Theo nodded sagely. 'Generally that's true, sir. You seem to be the lucky one. And nobody has contacted you yet about this?'

'No, this is the first I've heard from anybody since it got lifted! So how do I get it back? Is it in an impound lot or something?'

'It will be, sir, shortly. I suggest you check with the police department later today for information about how to get your car back. Thank you for your cooperation.' Theo handed back the paper and turned to head down the steps. He ignored Molino as he called out, 'But wait! What about . . . ?'

Theo ran it around in his head as he returned to his Navigator. It was as he'd figured. These guys *thought* they were pretty slick. It was a common practice to cruise a large parking lot, like an airport terminal, to boost a car to use, say, in a robbery. But a truly experienced booster would have gone to the long-term lot, where the owner might not return for days or even weeks, and there was less chance of the robbery being noted and reported. Molino's car had been reported within an hour or two of being taken. The odds were still against it being spotted immediately, but the risk of detection was much higher.

Theo was beginning to suspect he wasn't dealing with seasoned profession-als after all. There might only be two or three of them at most. Big Red had to have at least one accomplice, who had grabbed Vanessa while he distracted Darius, and who would be keeping her under wraps while Red did the footwork. There might be a third guy but he doubted there were more than that. His gut was telling him this was a small operation.

And at least one of them had an inside line to the organization.

He had a traitor on his hands.

★   ★   ★

'I didn't sleep last night, not a wink.' Lydia was frantically jamming clothing and other articles into the suitcase that lay open on the bed. 'Go on, drop her off, come back and get me, and let's get out of here!'

Brick yawned. He had finally nodded off, out of sheer exhaustion, early in the morning, but it seemed only a moment later that Lydia had shaken him awake. He had drowsily pulled some clothes out of a few drawers and had begun to pile

101

them into his own bag.

'Lemme go get us some coffee at least, something to keep our eyes open.'

She exhaled in exasperation. 'Coffee? Really?'

'I can't drive like this. I need caffeine.'

'If you really need to, but hurry. And *be careful.*'

Brick jammed his woolen cap over his tousled locks. 'I'll only be a few minutes. Whatta ya want, a latte?'

Lydia sighed. 'Just a strong coffee, with a lot of cream and sugar. Make it fast.'

Brick hustled up the driveway past the main house to the street, and turned right. There was a big coffee chain outlet at the corner where he could stay lost in the crowd that always inhabited the place. He'd be just another face among many. He stood in line, mumbled his order for two coffees and paid. The cashier asked his name and he hesitated and said, 'Joe,' and he was directed to another line to pick them up. As he reached for the cups, a young man grabbed one of them.

'Think that one's mine,' Brick told

him, pointing to the name written on the cup.

The younger man said, 'Oh, yeah. You're right. Sorry,' and handed him the cup.

Brick turned and elbowed his way out of the crowd, stopping to plop some cream and sugar into one of the cups before heading straight back home.

Lydia let him in and took one of the cups from him. 'You were crazy to go out,' she hissed. 'You and your caffeine! Are you sure nobody saw you?'

'Nobody paid any attention to me. I bought the coffee, I came back. I was just one more guy. I tell you, we're all right.'

She visibly softened as she spoke of their captive. 'She's all ready to go. I gave her breakfast and told her she'd be going home today, that she'll be back with her daddy soon.'

'Her daddy,' sighed Brick. 'Don't you think that's a little much?'

'That's how she thinks of him. She's such a sweetheart.'

'Yeah, sure. All right, let me get some of this coffee into my system and let it start working and then I'll make the drop-off. I still wish you'd do it.' He took a swig from his cup, not caring how the hot liquid burned his mouth.

'Hurry up. She's ready to go. I hope she'll be safe there until they come for her.'

'So that's the best place to leave her?'

'It'll be fine. They're very nice there.'

Again, Brick was amazed by the sweet and gentle side to this tough, hard woman. He was really growing fond of her, the whole package . . . the scary and the charming. They may not have gotten their money this time, but he had a feeling that, between both their sets of brains and ambition, they could pull some epic jobs together as a team: a regular modern-day Bonnie and Clyde. He hoped that while they made their escape, he'd have the opportunity to talk her into staying together. He'd like to stay with her as a team in more than one way.

'All right, let's do this.'

Lydia opened the door to the back room. Brick heard her speaking softly and a moment later walked out, leading a sleek, beautiful, pure white pitbull terrier on a leash, reaching down to pat it on its muscular neck.

'That's right, that's a good doggie, good Vanessa. We're going home now. You're going back home.'

Vanessa happily wagged her tail, and jumped up to lick Lydia's face. On her hind legs, she was eye to eye with her. Lydia laughed with delight. 'I'm gonna miss you too, sweetheart.'

She pulled a piece of paper out of her pocket and handed it to Brick. 'Here, I wrote it all down for you. The guy I found runs a small business called Waggin' Train. He does dog walking and dog sitting and accepts drop-ins. Right now he's got no other dogs, so he can accept Vanessa for up to six hours for thirty dollars. I told him that she'll be picked up by somebody named Robinson.' Brick nodded, a little impatiently. 'If he's willing to get paid when she's picked up, great. Otherwise, just pay him, don't make a fuss. As soon as you're on your way back, call me. We'll text Rybus how to get Vanessa back, but not until we're far away from here. I'll have the bags ready to toss in the car the moment you're back.'

Brick eyed the dog nervously. 'I'm really scared about this part. Can't we just let her loose or something?'

Lydia glared at him. 'Let her loose? What the hell is the matter with you?'

'Okay, okay. Why can't we just pack the car now and drop her off on the way?'

'No room in that tiny little car of yours.' She punched the words sarcastically. 'She even fit better in that Toyota. We've got a lot of bags and she's a lot of dog. Go, make it fast. I'll have everything ready by the time you get back.'

'You're sure he'll leave us alone once he's got her back?'

'I think so. I hope so.' Brick could tell from the look in her eye that she knew better. But they both needed to believe differently. It was their only hope.

Brick sighed. The faster he got this over with, the faster he and Lydia could be together and away from this very dangerous situation. He took the leash from her. 'Okay, come on, girl. Let's go to Doggie Day Care.'

Vanessa immediately crouched and began to growl, low and mean. Brick dropped the leash and stepped back. He and dogs did not get along very well.

'I don't think she likes me.'

'Can you blame her, the way you act around her? She doesn't like a lot of people in general, and she can tell when somebody's not being nice. Come on, girl, go with Brick, now.' She scratched the dog behind her ears.

Every time Brick approached, Vanessa growled, snarled, and even bared her fangs at him. Once she actually snapped her jaws at him.

'I can't help it. Pit bulls freak me out.'

'They're really nice dogs if they're raised right and not by jerks. She can sense your attitude.'

'I don't think I'm going anywhere with that dog. Maybe you better take her.'

Lydia exhaled impatiently. 'We have to get this over with and get out of here. All right, give me the keys to the car. I'll take her. You finish getting the bags packed. I'll be back as fast as I can.' She searched through the pile of clothes until she found a long-sleeved pullover, a floppy hat, and a pair of sunglasses. Covering herself to hopefully avoid detection, she picked up Vanessa's leash. Talking softly to the dog, Lydia led her out the front door, slamming it behind her.

Brick shook his head. None of this was working out the way he had planned.

★   ★   ★

The mood was somber around the table at the club. Theo stared at the other faces: Felix and four other members of the crew, desperate to figure out who Big Red was and where he might be found . . . and who his accomplices were.

Theo thought, *All this over a damned dog.* And he understood exactly why.

He remembered Yancey's wife, Mae: strikingly beautiful, brilliant, and as ruthless and intimidating as Rybus himself. They were an unbeatable team, and the organization's success owed as much to her as to him. They loved each other deeply, even as they presented a unified and formidable face to the world.

Then the brain aneurism had struck, swiftly, unexpectedly. Mae's sudden death cut Yancey to the quick. For an agonizing period it looked as if he would give up everything, fall to the jackals always waiting for the slightest sign of weakness, and take his crew with him.

Mae's last gift to Yancey had been the bull terrier puppy that became Vanessa. Yancey had transferred all his love to the animal almost immediately after Mae's passing. He rediscovered his vigor and his purpose and became even stronger. Vanessa accompanied him everywhere, and that had saved his sanity, his position . . . and, literally, his life.

Theo remembered that crazy dude Wally, who had become too fond of his own product . . . a tendency Theo tried to be careful to spot and weed out among his crew. He had decided there was something wrong with that guy, and his instincts had been right. One evening, zonked out of his mind, Wally had tried to approach Yancey in the crowded Hometown Club. He had a knife up his sleeve. The faithful pitbull had sensed something wrong and gone after him before he could harm his boss. What Vanessa left of Wally got turned over to Tiny shortly thereafter. His disappearance was never spoken of but served as a tacitly effective example to anyone in the organization who might consider disloyalty.

Yes, Yancey Rybus's companion animal was precious to him beyond words. He never remarried and didn't even seem to have any girlfriends. The kind of loyalty and simpatico that dog possessed substituted for any subsequent human companionship, it seemed. She was precious enough to lay out a million dollars to rescue, without hesitation.

Yancey now loved only money and Vanessa. Theo had to get that dog and that money back or there was going to be hell to pay.

His mind snapped back to the present.

'Word around,' Felix offered, 'is that there's someone like this guy who was doing some freelance work down the coast. Or trying to.'

'Where's this word from, exactly?' Theo asked.

'Couple guys I know downstate. Said he seemed full of it. Small-timer with lots of big talk.'

'Anybody come up with a name or anything?'

Felix shrugged his massive shoulders. 'He didn't make all that much of an impression. Just a story.' His phone began buzzing on the table and he answered it, speaking briefly.

'It's Nate. He thinks he saw Big Red just now.'

'What! Where?'

'Coffee joint on Shafford. Said he's pretty sure it looked like him.'

'Nate, who couldn't remember if the guy he saw was carrying a garbage bag or not, or even what color he was? Can we trust he's right this time?'

'Says he was wearing the dumb beanie. Red hair, scraggly beard. He followed him back down the street. Got an address. He's hanging nearby.'

Theo stood up. 'We got nothing better. Let's go check it out.'

★ ★ ★

Lydia couldn't help herself; she kept shaking her head and pursing her lips as she drove the green Honda Fit. Vanessa kept moving around in the back seat, looking out one window and then the other, obstructing her view in the rear-view mirror. What kind of a serious player drove a Honda Fit? His explanation was that it 'flies under the radar, not like those show boats that those gangsters are driving.' Actually, she had decided, it was all he could afford to drive. How she had gotten hooked up with this guy was beyond her. In the bar, he had talked a great game: never actually coming out and saying he had been CIA or military intelligence or something like that, but alluding to covert operations and dangerous acts. A regular real-life action figure. Even the name he went by, 'Brick,' sounded right, and fit him: big, red, and tough. She had been looking for a guy like that to help her with her own agenda. She had the inside knowledge and she figured he could supply the logistics, so to speak. He struck her as crazy and smart enough to help carry it out, but not so smart that she couldn't take advantage of him. The fact he clearly liked her was a plus, and she had played on that as well.

It had all seemed like a great plan, to both of them. Now things had taken a horrific turn and it all felt like a really bad mistake. She had known all along they were playing with maximally dangerous characters — she knew many of them, in fact — but she had been sure they'd go along and pay, and there would be enough of a window to get away before they could be found. Now Plan B was in effect: to drop off the dog and flee town as rapidly as possible, with nothing to show for it.

After which, she told herself, she would dump Brick, whom she increasingly thought of as a bad-luck charm as well as a bogus wannabe . . . but hopefully hang onto his lame car at least long enough to avoid notice and get to someplace safe to start a new life.

Something that at least made her feel slightly more comfortable was the presence of her 9mm Glock 19 automatic handgun in her bag. At least she could always count on that.

Waggin' Train occupied a storefront not far from a popular dog park. Lydia parked the car on the street nearby and led Vanessa out of the car. A young man behind the counter smiled toothily at her as they entered.

'You're the lady who called? Mrs. Robinson?' he asked. 'This must be Vanessa!'

Vanessa paused, tilted her head, and stared at the guy for a long moment. A low growl came from her throat. Lydia bent down and gently patted her on her side, speaking softly to her. 'Don't worry, it's gonna be fine. He's a friend.'

She told herself, *What did you expect? She's a gangster dog!* All Lydia needed was for the guy and Vanessa to get along for a short time. He knew what to do with dogs; if things got difficult, he wouldn't hurt her, just keep her isolated until Rybus came for her. And she knew that would be very soon, once Rybus knew where to find her.

The guy didn't seem to be concerned about Vanessa's unfriendliness. He just gushed kindness. 'I explained the process, right? She'll get a few hours to acclimate with us and see how we all do together. That's today's session. We like to see how she relates to other dogs, but at the moment we've got none here. We can do that later on. After that, we can talk about setting up a regular schedule for Vanessa's daycare.'

He came around the counter and bent down to talk to the dog. He was gentle and effective; she calmed considerably, and let him lightly scratch her behind the ears. Lydia quietly breathed a sigh of relief. All she wanted was to get this over with.

'We'll need for you to fill out some forms . . . information about Vanessa, basic background, that sort of thing.' He pointed to a clipboard on the counter. Lydia picked up the pen stuck into it and started filing it out with whatever might sound reasonable. None of it would matter once 'Mr. Robinson' came for the dog. The only thing she wrote down that wasn't a fabrication was the number of the burner phone they had sent to Rybus.

The guy gave her a copy of the form, which also included all the relevant information about rates and conditions.

She was surprised at how calm she remained and how well she thought she stayed in role, answering various questions with a smile and projecting an affection for the dog that at heart was real. The guy offered to give her a tour of the premises, and she knew that to stay in character she had to go along with it. Vanessa let the guy lead her on her leash to the dog exercise yard, and Lydia did her best to appear concerned, asking a lot of questions and making sure she came across as satisfied with the facilities. When she figured it was appropriate, she said, 'I think Vanessa's going to be very happy here. And I really have to get going.' The guy shook her hand and said, 'Thanks, Mrs. Robinson. Tell your husband he can pick up Vanessa this afternoon. He can pay us when he picks her up.'

She made a show of saying goodbye to the pit bull. She realized it wasn't all just a show. She liked dogs, probably better than people; she really was going to miss

Vanessa. For a gangster dog, she was truly a sweetheart, and must have been treated with kindness. Lydia knew way too many things about Rybus, truly nasty things, but to treat his dog with such affection, she mused, he couldn't have been all bad down to the bone. Go figure.

She forced herself to walk slowly out of the building and not sprint back to the Honda. She forced herself to focus, literally, on one step at a time: get back to the house, load the car, get out of town, contact Rybus, and don't look back. Later today she'd deal with the final steps: lose Brick, get far away . . . and never come back. She hoped by day's end she could close the book on all this. What a total mistake this whole thing had been.

She turned onto Shafford Avenue, a half block from their place. It was all she could do to keep herself from slamming on the brake and pulling a U-turn in a panic.

In the driveway leading to the back house there were two large dark vehicles: a Land Rover and a Lincoln Navigator.

She knew those cars.

117

Scarier yet, she knew that they'd know her.

She forced herself to breathe rhythmically through her pounding heart and to maintain her normal speed past the driveway. They didn't know the Honda. She wasn't recognizable with her big hat and sunglasses, and long sleeves covering her tats. She could drive by without being spotted. She could.

It was probably too late for Brick. But maybe they hadn't learned about her just yet and wouldn't be looking for her.

She didn't turn her head to look as she passed, but in her peripheral vision she saw a figure standing between the two SUVs, trying to look casual. He was one of the crew; he didn't seem familiar to her and hopefully she wasn't familiar to him either. He didn't seem to pay any special attention to her as she cruised by.

She was being so carefully nonchalant, she realized, that she wasn't paying attention to the street directly in front of her. She stopped for a tall skinny guy who emerged from behind a parked car and crossed Shafford right in front of her. He seemed nervous and preoccupied. He grinned in embarrassment and waved as he ran to the other side of the street. She was grateful she hadn't been going fast and hadn't had to slam on her brakes and call attention to herself.

She turned at the next intersection and as soon as she was halfway down the block, she gunned the engine.

She felt a twinge of regret for Brick. He may have been a dork, but she had come to have a *little* affection for the guy. But that was overshadowed by the sheer terror she was now beginning to feel at the realization that Rybus's crew *would* know, if they didn't already, that she was involved in this, no question about it. Brick didn't even have to talk; all they had to do was search the bags and find the passports.

That was the worst possible turn of events.

She had to get to somewhere safe and think. She had to assume that they'd ultimately know what kind of car she was driving too, so she'd unfortunately have to dump the Honda as well. But for now, her primary objective was to get to the freeway and get as far out of town as she could.

7

'You said she's *where*?'

Theo repeated the information into the phone to Rybus. 'She's at a dog day-care center by that big dog park. It's called Wagon Train or something like that.'

'So get somebody over there to pick her up, right now! And the guy who pulled this?'

'We got him right here. So far we can't get him to tell us anything besides where the dog was, but we will.'

'If you can't get it out of him, I'm sure Tiny can. And the money?'

Theo hesitated. 'Haven't found it yet. We're taking the place apart. He's gotta have partners in this. It must be with them. He'll give them up. I'll find the money, and I'll find them, all of them.'

'See that you do. And I want this guy, so keep him alive. I'll talk to you after I've got Vanessa back.' He broke the connection without allowing Theo to reply.

Theo sighed. All of this was not good. He was losing Rybus's confidence. The enterprise was in jeopardy. He had to find the money and get operations back on track. He had to find the rest of Big Red's crew.

The problem was, Big Red wasn't talking much. He kept claiming he didn't know anything, putting on a pretty convincing dumb-guy act. There were several ill-tempered individuals in the bedroom at the moment who hadn't been all that gentle with him, nor with his apartment, but it was to no avail so far. Theo was afraid to carry it too much further. He walked over to the chair where Brick was sitting, hands cuffed behind him. He swept his gaze around the room.

'This is it,' he said idly. 'This is where you took the photos of the dog.' He looked down at Brick. 'Listen, Red, this might be your last chance. Next stop for you is Yancey Rybus. Know what I'm saying here? I guarantee you, that's the last place you want to be. Tell me what I need to know and maybe I can save you a world of pain. Tell me who else is involved in this and *where's the money?* I gotta know where the money is.'

'There *is* no money!' Brick wailed. 'I told you! There was no money at the pickup! We got nothing!'

Theo stared thoughtfully at the terrified man. 'So you say. So who's this 'we' you're talking about? You're the only one taking the rap here.'

Brick clenched his jaw, glared up through a darkened eye at Theo, and said nothing else.

Felix walked into the bedroom, shaking his head. 'No money anywhere around here.'

'How about the burner phone? Find that?'

Felix gestured to Theo to follow him out to the front room. He spoke quietly as he reached into the pocket of his coat and withdrew two small folders and two booklets.

'No phone. I went through the bags. Just me, no one else. Found these.'

Two plane tickets to Mexico, and two passports. He opened them, read the names, studied the photos.

It was worse than he had thought. Much worse.

He had to keep Big Red away from Rybus as long as he possibly could . . . preferably for good.

'That was all I found with any ID.' Felix looked at Theo meaningfully. 'Nothing else in the bags tells any stories. Like I said, it was just me who looked.'

Theo nodded. He jammed the passports and tickets into his back pocket. Then he returned to the bedroom. 'Nate, come with me to get the dog. The rest of you, sit on this guy right here until you hear from me. No need to hurt him further, but keep him quiet. Nobody goes in or out, nobody knows he's here.' He turned back to Felix. 'Nobody talks to *anybody*.'

* * *

'You must be Mr. Robinson, here for Vanessa? You're really early!' The happy guy behind the counter looked downright disappointed. Theo put on his con-man's urban-hipster face, shrugged and smiled broadly.

'Yeah, I know. There's been a change of our plans and I needed to pick her up sooner.'

'She's doing great so far! Of course we have no other dogs here today, and your wife told me that Vanessa really hasn't been exposed much to other dogs, so we'll still have to try to see how she socializes, but she's such a sweetie, I don't think it's going to be a problem.'

Theo kept his beaming smile while he thought to himself: Yancey's pit bull is a 'sweetie'? Only the scariest man in the city could get away with that.

'I would have known you anywhere from your wife's description.' The guy placed a copy of the invoice on the counter. 'I'm afraid I still have to charge you the full amount.'

His wife. Man, the irony. He kept a straight face.

'That's no problem,' Theo said, looking

over the form. Earl and Nadine Robinson? He had to hand it to Lydia: she was creative. All the information on the paper was totally bogus, except, he noted, she had gone to the trouble to enter the real number of the burner they had sent to Yancey.

'I'll go get Vanessa. She'll be disappointed. She's having so much fun with the chew toys out there.'

Theo sighed and reached for his wallet.

When they reached the Hometown Club, Theo told Nate to bring the dog in and tell Yancey he was running down a crucial lead on the money and couldn't wait. He'd return as soon as he had more to report but he needed Nate back with him right away and that he'd need the dognappers' burner phone. Nate nervously led the pit bull out of the car and into the club, without incident; Vanessa was clearly happy to be back in familiar surroundings and trotted into the club ahead of Nate.

As Theo figured, Yancey was so delighted to have Vanessa back that he didn't immediately start to ask questions.

Nate was back out shortly and tossed the phone onto the passenger seat of the Navigator.

'Hop in,' he told Nate. 'I'm gonna drop you back with the others.' As he drove away, he considered that he didn't have much time before Yancey started asking *lots* of questions, and he didn't have any answers for them yet. He needed to keep Yancey isolated from anybody who could tell him anything until he could work this out.

After leaving Nate at the Shafford house, he drove his Navigator to Barlow Street near Lake Drive. He sat in his car, looking at the burner phone for a long time, then opened it and tapped out a text message, in full words.

LYDIA. THIS IS THEO. I HAVE THE BIG RED GUY. I HAVE THE DOG. I WILL FIND YOU. YOU KNOW THIS. RETURN THE MONEY AND I WON'T LOOK FOR YOU. IT'S YOUR ONLY CHANCE.

Of course that was nonsense. There was

no way he could let her go. And he didn't really think she'd give up the money. But he had to try. They had history; maybe she'd believe it.

It was only about a minute before the phone buzzed. He checked the screen.

WHAT RU TALKING ABOUT THERES NO MONEY. U LEFT US NOTHING.

He knew there weren't going to be any more messages, but he'd keep the phone handy, just in case. Before putting the phone in his pocket, he wiped the last exchange; Rybus could never see that one.

He got out and walked to Lake Drive, then paced around the bench before sitting on it, deep in thought.

Lydia had to have the money, didn't she? Or did she?

Was it possible that they were telling the truth, that they had never gotten their hands on the money?

That seemed crazy. There had only been about twenty minutes between the time he had dropped off the ransom and Big Red had driven to the pickup site. It was definitely him: not long after, they had seen him on the market surveillance camera. Theo himself had confirmed that the money was gone immediately afterwards. Where else could the money have gone in that short time?

Could Big Red possibly have been a diversion? Could Lydia — or someone else entirely — have done the actual pickup? How?

He rose and walked around, looking in every direction, including underneath the bench. He peered down the thick shrub-covered hill that dropped to the lake.

Was it his imagination, or did it look like somebody had climbed up or down through those bushes, even dragged something down there? Maybe it was just an animal, scrabbling through the undergrowth, but yes, there were bent and fallen branches and markings on the ground.

He carefully slid down the embankment, trying not to get scratched as he squeezed through the heavy foliage. There was a big tree at the base of the hill, along a deserted narrow path along the lakeside. He dusted off his shirt and pants and looked up and down along the lake. Someone could have been here last night . . . it was strange, but possible. A homeless guy? Someone looking for some kind of trouble, or trying to get away from trouble?

Or a confederate of Big Red's?

He saw the empty pint bottle, tucked into the bushes behind the tree, and picked it up. Someone had been here, and not all that long ago: the bottle was still clean. It was a cheap peach brandy, the label reading Sundown Premium.

He knew the store.

★　★　★

Theo put on his friendliest smile when he walked into Sundown Liquors and approached the man behind the counter. He had taken the time to don a pair of stage glasses and the squarest button-down shirt he could find, both courtesy of a thrift store on the next block. He had his story all set, delivered in his best urban-professional voice.

'So, my wife and I, we had this party last night, and one of the guests, I'm not sure which, had this amazing recipe for a punch that was supposed to use your own brand of peach brandy. It was the hit of the evening. I'd like to thank them and get the recipe, but I don't know who brought it. I thought maybe you might remember.'

The guy raised his eyebrows. 'That's a new one. Somebody actually did something good with that stuff? Usually we only sell a bottle now and then to some kid, or maybe somebody wanting to take some paint off the wall. Not too many people ever buy it. That musta been the park worker who came in here yesterday. Skinny guy, big nose, light brown hair? I don't know his name. He usually just buys a soda or a candy bar.'

'Now, that very well might be the person. Do you remember anything else about him . . . ?'

Not long afterwards, Theo was back at Brick's little back house. The guys in his crew, sitting around the front room, looked bored and expectant.

'Everything tight?' he asked Felix.

'Nice and quiet. Nobody in, nobody out. No calls. Big Red's not talking.'

'All right, then. I need you guys to clean this place up. Take everything and dump it securely. Then everybody clear out. I got a lot of stuff for you to get onto right away. I'll take Red over to Yancey.'

He spent the next few minutes running down a long list of items that needed to be dealt with, then told Felix to get everybody moving and to leave him and their captive alone in the back room. Felix gave him a look.

'You sure you gonna be okay?'

'No problem. Go on, get to it.'

Felix nodded, understanding all too well, and as he passed Theo, muttered quietly, 'You know where Tiny likes to leave his garbage, right? Seems nice and secure.'

132

A half hour later, Theo found himself in the back bedroom with Brick, still handcuffed to the chair, staring down at his feet. He pulled up a second chair, turned it around backwards, and straddled it, facing the redhead.

'Everybody treating you okay, Red? Or should I say Bradley?' He pronounced it with a comical drawl. 'That's your real name, right?'

'Nobody calls me that. They call me Brick.'

'Brick!' Theo shook his head and laughed. '*Brick!* Now if that doesn't just fit you! You're red like a brick. And seems you're smart as a brick too, Brick!'

'What are you waiting for, anyway? I know what's coming.'

'Now, see, I think it's a lot scarier to sit and *think* about what could happen. You know much history?'

'Little bit.'

Theo had an intimidating scowl that was all the worse for the fact his eyes, being two distinctly different shades, tended to be disconcerting. He turned it on now.

'Ever read about the Spanish Inquisition? Now, those were some bad dudes. They'd get their hands on a heretic, man, well . . . why do you think we talk about going medieval on someone? But first, they'd just lay out all those instruments and stuff, and just let the guy *look* at everything, let his imagination run, maybe for days. Sometimes that's all it took to get what they called a recanting, you know?'

'So you're trying to scare me into, what? I *am* scared. What can I tell you that you don't already know?'

'I know about Lydia. I don't think I know you. Nobody seems to know you. You from around here?'

'No. Chicago. I came out here last year, after I got out of the service. I freelanced down the coast for a while.'

Theo nodded. 'Here's what I figure. Lydia, you probably know she and I got history.'

Brick's eyes got wider. 'Look, we were just business partners, that's all. There was nothing between us. Honest. I slept out there, on the couch.'

Theo thought about that, looking around, and finally nodded. That was probably her idea, not his. The truth didn't matter in any case. 'She found you somewhere and invited you to come in on her plan, no doubt made it very enticing. I figure it was all her, you were just following the program. She's really the one behind all this, isn't she? She's the one I really want. Her and the money.'

'I keep telling you, there *is* no money! What kind of scam is this? Look, you're gonna kill me, go ahead and get it over with. I got nothing I can tell you. I don't know where she's gone and neither of us have any money.'

'So like they say on that quiz show: that your final answer?'

'There's no money! I swear!'

'Just curious. What'd you think you were going to do with it? You couldn't carry all that cash on the plane to Mexico with you.'

'I know a guy down the coast who was going to clean it and set up accounts for us. We'd be able to access the money from wherever we turned up.'

'Uh huh. That might even have worked.' Theo looked around the bedroom. 'Whose place is this, anyway? Not Lydia's.'

'We sublet this back house for two weeks online.'

A short-term internet lease! He couldn't help but laugh heartily. 'So how'd she and you . . . ' Theo moved his finger back and forth from Brick to empty space. ' . . . hook up on this scheme anyway, Bradley — excuse me, I mean Brick?' He snorted.

'I was trying to impress her in a bar. I told her I'd done all kinds of stuff in the military, like covert ops. She asked me if I was interested in something dangerous but profitable. She told me about Rybus and his dog and that he had a large amount of money available. I've run a few things like that and she sounded like she knew what she was talking about.'

'Sounds like you both fooled each other on that score, huh? So you put this lame plan together, distracting

Darius, snatching the dog, dropping off the burner phone, the whole bit? You took up with my ex-girlfriend and stole the most precious possession of the man who's everybody's worst nightmare, and figured *nothing could go wrong?*'

Brick by this point wasn't doing a great job of hiding his building terror. He understood it was bad for him, but it was beginning to dawn on him just how bad. 'Look, I'm telling you, there was no money. I saw an SUV drive through, I figured dropping off the money, but there was nothing at the drop point! Nothing! We were going to give up on getting anything and just run. The dog is safe. I don't know where Lydia went. She went to drop off the dog and never came back here. She probably saw you guys and bolted!'

'So what's she driving, another stolen hunk of junk like that Toyota you stole? Slick move, by the way, losing us at the market. I gotta give you that.'

'She's got my car. She could be anywhere by now. It's a Honda Fit.'

'A Honda . . . ' Theo couldn't help

starting to laugh again. 'A Honda Fit. Couldn't find a skateboard? You some gangster, all right. You know, *Brick*, I'm beginning to believe you really *didn't* get any money.'

Theo sat in thought for what must have felt like an eternity to the terrified Brick, then sighed deeply.

'You caused a lot of people a lot of trouble, you know? Yancey Rybus doesn't tolerate minor annoyances, much less something on this scale. He's already tended to Darius just for losing the dog, and for you ... he's got something special in mind.' He stood up. 'But Yancey isn't who you're talking to, lucky for you, and I need you to disappear, completely. Can you do that?'

'Yes!' Brick coughed. 'Yes I can! Absolutely!'

'Okay.' Theo pulled a small key out of his short pocket and walked around behind Brick, unlocking the handcuffs. Brick looked up at him in surprise. 'Go on. There's the door. You better get outa here before I change my mind.'

There was no clue to be found in

Theo's unwavering smile as to what might be going on in his head at that moment.

8

Starting work Wednesday morning, Marlon was amazed to find an email notification from SID confirming an ID on his victim: one Darius Mitchell, twenty-four, who had been in the system since age sixteen with various minor offenses. There was nothing new on his record for the past three years; apparently he had been keeping his nose clean. No current next-of-kin was provided, which meant some work to root out his background. Marlon sighed. He reached for his buzzing desk phone.

'This is Logan in Property. We got a guy here who says he knows you and wants to talk to you.'

'Really. Who is he?'

'His name's Lorenzo Boggs. We picked him up for B&E. You know him?'

'Yeah, unfortunately I do. I'll be right up.'

Property Crimes' interview rooms

weren't any nicer than those in Personal Crimes, but Marlon did note this one still smelled of a recent paint job, in a reasonably neutral green.

'So Bogo, just why am I here exactly?'

A downcast Boggs gazed with heavy-lidded eyes at Marlon. 'I figured since you and me go back,' he droned lazily, 'you might be able to help me out here. I got myself into a bad rap with these guys.'

'Uh . . . you got picked up at your apartment with stolen property on the premises.'

'Okay, okay. I got something I can trade if you can help me out.'

'Burglary isn't my department. I'm robbery and homicide. What is it you think you've got that can help me?' Boggs had been a useful confidential informant to Marlon a few times but somehow he didn't see what he could offer just now.

'I think I saw something go down last Sunday. I was hanging out over on Croftworth Way, by the university.'

'You mean you were casing an electronics store that was closed for the day. The one you broke into later.'

Boggs waved a hand in dismissal. 'Whatever. My point is, I was kinda standing around and must not have been, whattaya call it, conspicuous, and I happened to look across the street, where the sidewalk goes along the campus there, and I think I saw a kidnapping.'

'A kidnapping. Really.'

'Well . . . actually more like a dognapping. There was this guy, walking this great big white dog, like a pit bull, and these two folks ran a number on him. One of them was walking towards him with a big pile of boxes, and he made a point to stumble into him and knock him over and drop the boxes on him, while this woman, I think, came out of the bushes and grabbed the dog's leash, then led it back behind the bushes. While the dog dude was trying to sort himself out, the first guy got up and ran back and jumped in a car and drove off. I'm guessing his partner doubled around and he picked her up down the street with the dog.'

'A dognapping. That's what you got for me.'

142

'Hey, it looked like an expensive dog! It was clearly a set-up! The two dognappers were both covered up in coats and hats and shades. The guy with the boxes was this big dude, with a scraggly red beard. The guy walking the dog looked like some kinda gangster or something, with these bright blue star tats on his neck, I could see 'em all the way across the street . . . ' Boggs pointed to the side of his throat.

'Wait a minute. Tell me more about the guy with the tats.'

Boggs wasn't able to tell him much more.

Marlon said he'd see if anyone had reported a stolen dog, but otherwise, he doubted this was anything he was able to follow up on. He did promise to at least talk to the detectives who had picked up Boggs. He might have actually been of some help.

Back at his desk, he considered what Boggs had told him. The guy with the dog sure sounded like Darius Mitchell, but how could he use that?

His phone buzzed again.

'Marlon, it's Gene. Wanted to check in with you on that DB you pulled yesterday. Any word yet?'

Marlon rolled his eyes and exhaled. 'Just a name so far. Darius Mitchell. Minor record. That mean anything to you?'

'Nope. I'll look into it. I'm still thinking this has something to do with Yancey Rybus.' There was a pause as Hogan waited for him to come back with some further tidbit for him. He didn't bite.

'Well, let me know if you come up with anything, Gene. One other thing. Would it mean anything to you if there was a big dog connected to any of this somehow?'

'A big dog? What do you mean?'

'I happened to hear about a guy who looked like Mitchell, something about a dog he was seen walking. Big white dog, like a pit bull maybe.'

'I've got no idea what you're talking about, Marlon. Talk to you later.'

The phone started buzzing again almost immediately. Marlon cussed under his breath and picked it up.

'Is this Detective Morrison, who's

handling the death on Blaisdell Drive?'

Marlon sighed heavily and sat back in his chair. 'Yes, it is.'

'I'm with Public Works. We got sent up to clean out the dump site this morning and, well, I'm afraid we've got two more bodies for you.'

'Two? Up in the state park?'

'No, just below the park, still inside the city limit. Our crew was clearing the area where furniture and other trash had been left. We found two more dead bodies. Same place.'

When it rained, Marlon considered, it certainly poured. He rubbed his eyes. 'Okay. I'm on my way.'

*　*　*

Sela Hovsepian was once again on the scene, along with an SID crew. Marlon watched as they carefully opened a large deteriorating wooden cabinet and withdrew a dark vinyl body bag. They laid the bag out on the ground and started unzipping it. More SID techs were busy with shovels, uncovering a chest that had

145

been partially buried in debris. Before long they were looking down at two bodies, laid out on the ground side by side. Sela began to unwrap the older one, which had been left in an identical state to the body they found yesterday, stripped of clothing and swathed in heavy plastic sheeting. The smell was again overpowering to Marlon; he could never figure how the coroners and techs were able to work around such a stench.

'This one's been here quite a while, maybe some months. The other one, though . . . he looks as if he's brand new. I'll be able to tell better shortly but I'm guessing he's been dead less than twenty-four hours.' After a while she gave up trying to unwrap the older body. 'I'll need to have him transported to the examination area where I can do it with care. I can probably tell you more about the newer one.'

The newer victim, cheekbones darkly bruised, still looked as if he might open his puffy eyelids and stand up at any moment. He was a tall man with red hair and scraggly beard, dressed in a dark

T-shirt and pants. Hovsepian bent over the newly deceased, rolled him over and pointed to the holes and dark stains in the shirt. 'He was shot three times in the neck and back, at fairly close range. But judging from the ligature marks on his wrists and the marks on his face, he was handcuffed and beaten first.'

Marlon stood up and looked around at the large hillside space that had been turned into a de facto dumping ground, marred by mounds and mounds of old furniture, appliances, and detritus. The five-member maintenance crew that had been sent there that morning had barely scratched the surface of the place.

'What are the odds there are more body dumps here?' he asked Hovsepian.

'Who knows? It's overlooked and disregarded. Nobody wants to claim this. It's city land but they want to pretend it's state park, and the state wants nothing to do with it.'

Marlon went through the implications of what he was now considering. The upper echelons of the department and the city were never happy when a bunch of new murders were found. It was more work and reflected badly on them politically. It was never about solving crime to the mucky-mucks; it was about public perception and the avoidance of more hours and dollars. Marlon tended to avoid all of that himself. He just wanted to stay unnoticed, finish out his run and retire. He should let it all lie.

You're usually looking for the least possible amount of work, Hogan had said. Maybe that was true, but it rankled when his incompetent fool ex-partner had said it so matter-of-factly, like it was his commonly accepted reputation.

He made up his mind and got on his phone to his lieutenant and laid out what he wanted done.

'Marlon, are you sure about this? Sweep that whole area? Are you sure?'

Castillo knew the implications as well, whether or not anything ultimately was found here. Marlon also figured his lieutenant had wanted to say, 'You're making yourself a lot more work, what's the matter with you?' but was being tactful.

Something inside him just hollered *enough*!

'I'm sure, Lou.'

Castillo's deep sigh was clearly audible over the phone. 'All right, then. This better be worth it, for your sake and mine as well.'

★   ★   ★

'I talked to a police officer the other day. Now they send a detective? I'm impressed, but for what good is it?'

Spiros Pappas, operator of Spiros' Cigar Lounge, was an energetic man in his sixties. Marlon, who had given up smoking a year before, couldn't take the reek and the haze in the lounge, filled with about a dozen cigar smokers, all men, so he had asked the proprietor to come out on the street. Pappas was still redolent of tobacco. Marlon figured it was in the guy's skin by now. The older man gestured at a table set up outside his lounge with piles of lacquered wooden cigar boxes and a sign that read ONLY $3 EACH.

'Look at these things, they're beautiful, aren't they? Lovely works of art. They still care about the craft in some of the places we import these from: Europe, Latin America. After we sell the cigars, it's a shame to waste them, so I put them out for sale. People buy them for jewelry boxes, for all sorts of things.'

'So last Sunday, some guy just grabbed up the whole table of boxes and ran?'

'Yeah, is that crazy? He stopped and looked in the window, kinda suspicious, then just started scooping up all the boxes and took off with armfuls of them. I saw him through the window and came out, but he was way down the street and I wasn't gonna chase him and leave the lounge unattended. So I called the cops and they sent a uniform over who took a report.' Pappas shrugged. 'I don't really expect anything gonna come of it, but it was my, whattayacall it, civic duty, you know?'

'And did you see what this guy looked like?'

'Kinda. Big guy, in a long dark coat, and one of those wool hats like sailors wear. Which was odd because it was really warm Sunday. I even had the air conditioning on. He bent over to look in the display window, which as you can see is tinted so it's hard to see inside, and that's when I got a look at him. He had this messy red beard and hair sticking out from under the hat.'

'And he took off that way, you said, right?' Marlon jerked a thumb.

Pappas nodded. 'Weird thing was, not long after, I found my boxes scattered all over the street around the corner, across from the university! I walked over and picked up a few of 'em. Some got broken or maybe picked up by people passing by. I mean, we're not even talking a hundred dollars' worth of merchandise there, stuff I otherwise woulda just thrown out. It's no big deal. So whatta ya gonna tell me, you actually gonna find this guy?'

Marlon opened his phone and brought up one of the pictures he had just taken of the newly found murder victim. 'Could this be the guy?'

Pappas peered at it. 'Uh . . . maybe. The beard looks right. Is this guy *dead*?'

'Afraid so. But you might be of help to me in finding who killed him.'

'*Den to pistevo!* He was a bum, but to get killed? That's a shame!'

Marlon stared down the street, to the intersection of Croftworth Way at the campus border. Two of his vics had apparently crossed paths there on Sunday, and now both were dead. A third person, probably a woman, was also involved. There was a narrative forming here. He just had no idea yet what it could be.

His phone buzzed. It was Lieutenant Castillo.

'Marlon, I know you're caught up with those new vics, but when you're free, I need you to follow up on a call we just got about a robbery assault from Monday at a market called Stop'n'Shop. I've got nobody else here to do it. It shouldn't take you too long.'

'This happened two days ago and they're just reporting it?' Marlon wasn't happy to hear the address, which was some distance away, near the Aquatic Park. But there was no arguing with the

Lou. He pocketed the phone and murmured, 'Stop'n'Shop, great.'

★   ★   ★

'So let me get this straight, Mrs. Lin. Your husband here was robbed and assaulted Monday night?'

Tom Lin, a weary middle-aged man, rolled his eyes and shook his head. He was leaning on the counter while his wife stood beside him, arms folded, jaw set. 'She's making a big deal of this. They didn't rob me and they didn't assault me.'

'They forced you to go into the back room. They stole the security video disc.' Betty Lin glared at him and then back at Marlon. 'They could have killed him!'

'You weren't even here, Betty!'

Marlon sighed, marveling at his bad luck in pulling these two. 'So, Mr. Lin, explain to me exactly what did happen Monday night.'

'These two big guys came in looking for the tall red-haired guy, so . . . '

'Wait. Tall red-haired guy?'

'Yeah, the one that ran through the

153

store a few minutes before that. He came in from the parking lot and ran out the back. The two guys wanted to see the footage on the camera, to see if there were shots of him. When they saw him, they made me make a disc copy that they took. Then they left.'

'They were gangsters!' Betty yelled. 'They could have killed you!'

'They were scary guys.' Tom nodded. 'You could say they threatened me, sure. But they stayed cool. I did what they wanted and they didn't hurt me. But they did say not to tell anybody about them.' He returned his own glare at Betty and then at Marlon. 'Especially not cops. Now maybe I *am* in trouble!'

'They probably also stole the car that was in the lot,' Betty said.

Marlon wiped his forehead. 'What stolen car was that?'

'Abandoned in the parking lot end of the night. We called the police when we were closing up. You don't know about the stolen car?'

'No, ma'am, that would be Property Crimes, another department. The city has

154

maybe four or five car thefts a day.'

'They stole a car, they threatened my husband, they took a video disc! What are you going to do about this?'

Tom Lin shrugged apologetically to Marlon as if he wanted nothing to do with this. Marlon felt much the same. But he had to at least go through the motions. It was wasted time, taking him off the trail of the case that interested him.

Or was it?

'So tell me you haven't recorded over the original video that these two guys wanted so badly to see, the one of the red-haired guy?'

'Are you kidding? My wife wouldn't let me!' He motioned for Marlon to follow him into the back room.

It wasn't much of a shot, just a few seconds of a man's head as he ran past the camera. Marlon had him rerun it over a few times, then had him freeze a frame. He opened his camera and brought up the photograph of the morning's victim and stared back and forth between the two.

'How high is that camera? How tall

155

would a guy have to be to be photographed like that?'

'Maybe six feet, a little more.'

'What do you think, could this be the same guy?' He showed the phone photo to the Lins.

'Maybe, hard to say.'

Marlon wasn't sure what was going on but his luck was running crazy today. What were the odds that the guy on the footage was his vic?

He generally scoffed at those touchy-feely New Age types, but damned if it wasn't like the universe was trying to tell him something.

'So tell me more about the two gangsters, would you?'

'They were both dark. The one guy was darker, and really big. He had, like, what do you call them, cornrows in his hair? And one of those little hats with the brim. The other guy was lighter, less tall, well built.' He pointed to his left eye. 'And he had one eye that was lighter than the other. It was, like, grey. The other was dark brown. It was creepy.'

★　★　★

A couple of phone calls later, Marlon was able to speak with the overworked-sounding detective in Property Crimes who had been assigned the stolen car. The owner, Luis Molino, had actually already been in touch with her, which surprised Marlon. He had come in the previous night to fill out the necessary forms and had been referred to the impound lot. Things did not usually happen that fast. She gave him Molino's contact information, and he tapped another number into his phone.

'You the detective I spoke to yesterday?' Luis began after Marlon had introduced himself. 'I'm going to go pick up my car after work today! Appreciate the fact you guys found it so fast. I mean, three days is pretty good, right?'

'Uh . . . not me, sir, it must have been someone else who you spoke with.'

'The Grand Theft Auto guy, the undercover detective, you know him?'

Marlon pinched the bridge of his nose and shook his head. There was no such thing as a Grand Theft Auto detail in the department. Individual car thefts went through Property Crimes. 'He identified himself as a detective, did he? Did he give you a name or show you any ID?'

'He flashed something at me, but he just sounded right, you know? He knew about my car and who I was and everything. I figured he was okay.'

'What did he look like?'

'Kinda tall guy, dark, in a black T-shirt and slacks. Seemed pretty smart, all business. Oh . . . and I couldn't help noticing, one of his eyes was like hazel-colored and the other was dark brown.'

'And your car was stolen when?'

'Last Saturday, from the airport. You don't know this whole story? Don't you guys talk to each other?'

'I'm afraid sometimes it's one hand not talking to the other, you're right. Mr. Molino, was the registration in the car when it was stolen?'

'Sure, in the glove compartment.'

Property Crimes had mentioned there was no registration form in the Toyota;

they had matched the owner's ID off the VIN, the vehicle identification number. The guy impersonating a detective conceivably had taken the registration from the car and located Molino that way.

'So please tell me, exactly what time and from which parking lot your car was stolen?'

Marlon was not happy about having to drive to the airport but he knew that there would be security footage in the parking lot and that there was no way the overtaxed Personal Crimes Department would get to it for some time yet. Thirty minutes of congested traffic later, he was in a security supervisor's office staring at a monitor. It was a comparatively short period during which Molino's Toyota could have been boosted so they didn't have to wait long before he saw what he had come to see.

It was a tall guy in a wool beanie and a long dark jacket, walking furtively up the incline of the structure and stopping behind the Toyota. He looked right and left, then walked to the driver's side of the car. From under his coat he slid out a familiar long tool, again scanning about him, then turned his attention to the door.

'A Slim Jim,' Marlon muttered. 'There, he's popping the door. Now he'll hotwire it. That's gotta be my man. Can you back up and freeze a frame on him and blow it up?'

The video was black and white and not high resolution, but it was good enough. The weird luck of the day was holding: the car thief, he was sure, was his murder victim.

He made more calls. Luis Molino wasn't going to be picking up his car from the impound lot today after all. SID would be doing that instead.

The traffic had only gotten worse for the return drive to the unit. Surprisingly, Marlon didn't find it all that irritating; he remained lost in thought for most of the trip. Back at his desk, he grabbed his phone and dialed Gene Gehm.

'Marlon, nice to hear from you. Have you got something for me?'

'I'm hoping you've got something for me, Gene. Any luck on Darius Mitchell?'

'Nothing to speak of. It seems he was a low-level member of one of Rybus's crews. Kind of a gofer. Nobody here seems to know much more about him. How he turned up dead, nobody here's got a clue.'

'And nothing about a dog?'

'A dog? I don't know.'

'How about this: do you know anything about a guy with one hazel eye and one brown eye?'

'That sounds like Theo Charles, Rybus's right-hand man. What about him?'

'What's this Theo look like?'

'Tall dude, thirties, well built, short dark hair. Smart, charming, but a nasty piece of work. He's the fixer and the arranger. They call him T.C. How's he involved in this?' He sounded suddenly eager.

'I'm not sure yet. I'll get back to you.'

Moments after closing the call to a distinctly disappointed Gene, Marlon's phone was buzzing again. It was getting tiring; his phone hadn't had this much activity in a long time.

'Detective Morrison, this is Jameson in the SID Crime Lab. I was asked to call you by Sela Hovsepian over at the coroner's office.'

'You were? I mean . . . she did?'

'I don't know what you did to impress her so strongly, but she must really think you're on the ball. She asked if I could at least expedite the fingerprints on your two victims from this morning, and then give you a call right away if we found anything.'

'So, do I take it you found something?'

'Nothing as yet on the older body. But we got an immediate hit on the more recently deceased on IAFIS.'

IAFIS, the FBI's national fingerprint resource, was often promoted as being able to give results to law enforcement agencies in less than a half hour. Marlon's experience was that it usually took somewhat longer. For some reason, today everything was just dropping into his lap.

'Former serviceman, name Bradley Brixton. He was discharged from the army about a year ago. I can send you over the information, but you're going to have to wait on any further forensic results. There was only so much I could speed up here.'

Marlon thanked him and hung up. He was exhausted but he didn't want to stop just yet. He turned to his computer.

Jameson's email appeared almost immediately. He followed the links to Brixton's army records, which were unremarkable: he had gone in as a private and left as one via a medical discharge. Marlon scrolled until he found telephone numbers and began jotting them down on a yellow legal pad he pulled from a nearby desk. He often made fun of one of his old school colleagues, Frank Vandegraf, for constantly using those yellow pads, but he had to admit, it proved an effective way to organize his thoughts.

It took him four calls to finally get a contact number for what was apparently Brixton's closest next-of-kin: his sister, Alannah Brixton O'Rourke. He took a deep breath and wiped his forehead. He had never forgotten how much this kind of scut work took out of him, and he was only getting older and less tolerant of it all. Gene Hogan's words about making too much work for himself came back to him once again and he felt his anger rising. He stabbed the sister's number into his desk phone.

Alannah herself answered the phone, her hoarse voice sounding harried and distracted. Marlon could hear kids screaming and crying in the background. It sounded like an infernal circus to him; just how many kids did she have there anyway? He had never warmed to little kids, never had any of his own. Just another involvement.

There were lots of things Marlon hated about his job, but one of the worst was informing anyone of the violent death of a loved one. He identified himself and stuttered through what he hoped was a reasonably gentle revelation, then waited for a long time while all he could hear were the kids, then Alannah's voice in a whisper telling them to quiet down, one by one. Finally she came back on the line, with an audible sniff. 'Oh my God. Brad? Oh my God.' There was another long pause and her voice regained control. This was one strong and self-possessed woman, Marlon decided, and felt grateful that she might make his job easier than he had anticipated.

'What happened to him?'

'I'm working on figuring that out, ma'am. He was just discovered yesterday. He was shot to death. I'm afraid I don't have too many details just yet. I was hoping you might be able to help me.'

'We weren't that close. I don't think Brad was ever close to anybody. When he got out of the army last year, he drifted around. I think he got involved in some fairly shady dealings here and there. He didn't talk about his life and that was fine by me. I didn't want to know. He asked me if we could be what he called his mail stop.'

'I see he had a medical discharge.'

'Yeah. Damn fool shot himself in the foot. He always thought he was going to be some kind of Ranger or Special Forces guy, but the motor pool was the best he could do. He never even got a stripe. Anyway, he was getting checks here until he decided to move out your way. Then we started forwarding them to him. And sometimes he'd hit us up for a 'loan' as well.'

'So . . . you have an address around here where you were sending them?'

'Sure. In fact he called me just last week and gave me a new one. He said it would be only temporary. He was about to start a great new job. He couldn't tell me any details because it was 'sensitive.' But he was going to be traveling and would be paid a lot and might not be able to be found for quite a while.' She actually snorted into the phone. 'Tried to make it sound like more of his Special Ops pipe dreams. I figured that was more blue sky stuff. He probably got in some trouble there, like with some woman, and had to go on the run, and it caught up with him. That would have been just like him.' She went quiet for a long beat. 'Oh my God, listen to me. You must think I'm terrible. Here I am, talking trash about my dead brother. But that's how he was.'

'No, it's perfectly understandable, Mrs. O'Rourke. I get it, believe me. So you've

166

got an address for him that you got only last week?'

Marlon tried to contain his excitement as he tried to politely finish the conversation, explaining there was an autopsy and inquest in progress, promising to inform her when and how she could claim her brother's remains. Ms. O'Rourke remained stoic throughout. He stumbled through some ritual condolences and finally broke the connection.

He looked down at the yellow pad where he'd written the address and had circled it so many times that the ballpoint pen had dug through to the sheets beneath.

Marlon sat back in his chair, hand over his eyes, breathing deeply. He couldn't believe how tired he felt. He glanced at his watch. Was it really only 3:30? It felt like midnight.

At the beginning of this week, he had come to work with only one goal in mind: to keep things on as even a keel as possible, to make no waves. Whatever cases were on his desk, he would, as usual, let them unfold at their own pace and conserve his energy in dealing with them. But then things just started falling out of the sky, and he actually got caught up in them. Was it a moment's insanity, for him to start getting seriously proactive on these new cases? He hadn't put out this much energy at work in ages, and for good reason. He saw how things always seemed to come back to bite him when he did. Odds were he was going to regret it this time.

But the craziest thing, he realized, was that he was actually getting a charge out of all this, the thrill of the chase, the challenge of fitting the parts together.

He was actually enjoying it.

He ripped the page off of the yellow pad, folded it up and stuck it in his sports coat pocket, and rose from his chair. The day was not over just yet.

★ ★ ★

The block of Shafford Avenue consisted of residential homes. Many of the garages behind the main house had clearly been converted into a second smaller house, known to builders as a 'mother-in-law unit' or 'granny unit,' as a source of extra income for the owners. Marlon double-checked the address on his paper, rang the front doorbell and got no answer. He strolled around the side of the property and saw several plastic garbage cans. The lid of one could not completely close because the can was so full. He noted a large crumpled-up empty dog food bag among other items. This Brixton guy seemed to have some connection with dogs, all right. He walked down the driveway to the back unit and knocked. The house was dark, but the blinds were up. The unit held furniture but no other evident signs of occupancy; it looked cleaned and vacated.

He was walking back up the driveway to the street when he heard the commotion: the squeal of tires, the slam of a car door, the unmistakable *pop* of a gunshot, then the unbelievably loud and intense shriek of a woman.

He ran to Shafford and looked up the block, where a large late-model SUV had stopped in the middle of the street and

169

several people had converged. He saw weapons.

He was on the phone with a shots fired/need backup alarm, stressing there were multiple shooters, then pulled his own service weapon out of his shoulder holster and headed up the street at as fast a trot as his weary aging legs could muster.

'This,' he told himself, 'is exactly what I did not want to happen to me in my home stretch.'

9

It was Otis Wilson's favorite time of the day at the Aquatic Park: Wednesday midmorning, and nobody around yet to start littering again. Weekday visitors didn't usually start showing up until early afternoon. There was just him, his rake and bag, and the waterfowl, scouring the grounds looking for scraps of food left by those eating outdoors the day before.

Actually, there was one other person: a tired-looking guy with his hands in his pockets strolling along the lake shore towards him, a friendly smile on his face. When he was in hailing distance, he held a hand out to Otis.

'Excuse me, sir, I'm hoping you can help me. I'm looking for a guy who works here in the park. Skinny guy, kinda big nose, mussy light brown hair?'

Otis stopped and laid his bag down, and a smile came to his own face. 'That sounds to me like Web. Web Musgrave.

Only one I can think of who matches that description.'

'If you say so. Any idea where I can find him?'

'Well, I'm afraid the word I got this morning is that Web is no longer with Parks, Rec and Waterfront. He parted company with us yesterday.'

The stranger looked disappointed. 'I'm sorry to hear that. The other day, my wife left her bag here in the park. She's kind of ditzy like that, you know?' He rolled his eyes and grinned wryly. 'That guy, Web you say is his name? He saw what happened and ran after us, maybe a block or so, to return it. We would have driven ten miles home and she would have had a heart attack when she realized she had left it. I really wanted to find him and thank him. And give him a reward.'

'Web did that? Good for him. Well . . . I'm not supposed to tell you this, but I guess it's okay. I know that he lives somewhere over on Shafford, you know where that is?'

'Shafford?' The guy looked stunned, like he had been hit by something, then quickly recovered his composure. 'Get out! Sure, I . . . know friends on that street! And you say his name is Web Musgrave?'

'Web as in Webster. Right. You oughta be able to find him.'

'I should say so. Thank you, sir, thank you so much. You'll make my wife Linda very happy.' The guy gave Otis a final parting smile and turned around and trotted off down the path back to the parking lot.

Otis returned to his rake with his own smile, pleased that a nice guy like Webster was going to get a reward he richly deserved.

⋆　⋆　⋆

Back at his car, Theo stifled a yawn and looked at his phone as it buzzed one more time. Yancey. He let it go to voice mail again. He still wasn't ready to talk to him but knew he couldn't avoid him indefinitely. He'd have to explain the absence of both Big Red and the money. Yancey was no fool; by now he'd also concluded

that this all came from someone within his organization, who knew there was ready cash on hand, Vanessa's importance to Yancey, and where and how to find her in a vulnerable spot.

Theo knew all that, and was the last one to have the money in his possession. It wasn't a good spot to be in. Another sleepless night of frenetic activity had just added to the anxiety.

The phone started buzzing again. This time it was Felix. He thumbed the answer button on the screen.

'Yeah, what's up?'

'You know that Yancey's looking for you, right? Been calling all of us all morning. We all told him we don't know where you are but you must be taking care of business.'

'I'll tend to that. Anything new on the girl?'

'I got a few of the crew looking for the Honda. I haven't told anyone who she is, just that it's a girl. If anybody does find her, then we need damage control.'

'We'll deal with that if it happens. Important thing is to find her.'

'Okay, T.C. But you better deal with Yancey. Soon he's gonna start in on the rest of us, and you know where that could lead.'

Theo ended the call and sat back in the driver's seat of the Navigator. He couldn't stop now, with too much on the line, but man, was he tired. Wiping down the apartment thoroughly, bagging and lugging the body, depositing it up on the hillside, then cleaning out his car — that was all hard work, done painstakingly and exactingly. He normally avoided the recreational stimulants that were a major stock of his trade, save for a special occasion. It had been made clear to him how guys in the crew who got caught up in that started showing lapses in judgment, like Wally. Others had also been taken into the back room by Tiny and had ended up where he had put Big Red last night. But he had needed to keep himself going for too many hours now, so he'd broken his own rule . . . and now everything was wearing off. He closed his eyes. He just needed to catch his breath for one small second.

The buzzing of his phone brought him back. He felt sludgy; how long had he fallen asleep? More than two hours?

'T.C., it's Felix. We got trouble. Yancey's got Nate. He's having a serious conversation with him up in the office.'

Theo shook his head, trying to clear his brain. He realized he had crashed, heavily.

Felix continued, 'Man, Nate's just a kid. He doesn't know better. They probably won't even have to scare him much. He's gonna tell Yancey everything.'

'Okay, listen. Nate doesn't know about Lydia, right? You and I are the only ones who know she's involved. Any luck finding her?'

'Nada, man. She's up in smoke.'

'All right. I gotta do a couple things quick, then I need you to meet me over on Shafford. I'll call you with the exact address.'

'Back on Shafford, where we were yesterday? Is that wise, man?'

'I think the money's there. We have to find the money. I'll call you within the hour. Meanwhile, stay low. Don't talk to anybody else. Don't let Yancey find you too.'

He saw his phone was about to die, and he had been so distracted he hadn't brought a charge cord in the car. He had a crib on the other side of town that he kept secret from everybody, even Yancey, that came in handy for clandestine stopovers and confidential storage. It was quiet and had underground parking, away from passing eyes. He had a laptop computer there; with any kind of luck, this Webster's name and street should yield him an address on one of the directory sites. He could charge his phone, even take a quick shower and change clothes so he didn't feel quite so rangy. He figured it might be a while before he could do that again. He could be ready to go within the hour he had promised Felix.

Theo started up his Navigator, muttering disjointedly to himself.

He arrived at the apartment complex in decent time and turned into the underground garage. In his apartment, he figured he was safe for a while at least.

The first thing he did was to plug his phone into the charger. Finding Musgrave's address on his laptop turned out to be a bit more difficult than he had anticipated. He was old enough to remember, as a kid, the ubiquitous telephone books that also listed street addresses; in fact he remembered his mother brandishing one of those thick books at him when he got out of line. Now telephone directories were a rarity, and it was increasingly difficult to track down a phone number, much less an address, on public internet sources. He finally entered a credit card number to pay the requisite ten dollars to access a private 'white pages' site and found the street address he wanted. After a quick shower and change of clothes, he double-checked his Desert Eagle semi-automatic pistol to insure it was fully loaded, and grabbed an extra magazine of ammunition to have handy just in case.

He was still angry with himself for crashing the way he had. His life was on the line here and he had to keep going. He opened a drawer and pulled out a small vial of crystal powder for a quick pick-me-up, then dialed Felix and told him the Shafford address.

'T.C., are you sure? That's like right down the block from . . . '

'I'm sure. Just be there. Stay low and wait for me.'

★   ★   ★

Lydia kept telling herself this was crazy . . . totally bat-crazy. She should have kept running south. By the time she had driven down the coast a short distance, she had thought out a plan. She had first stopped at a remote location of her bank and cashed out her substantial account. When Theo had told her he was tired of her, he had given her what he considered a generous parting gift, along with a clear message that she'd better never come asking for more. He had correctly judged her to be the type that wasn't going to go talking publicly about him or his business. What he had not correctly judged was how personally she took rejection or how much her definition of

179

'generous' differed from his own.

There were other things Theo hadn't judged correctly about his former girlfriend: for example, how sharp and observant she had been, taking in all the information around her, snippets of conversation, notes carelessly left for a few seconds too long, and putting them together to understand how the organization worked. Nor had he properly estimated the level of greed she harbored. She wanted her vengeance, yes, but she also wanted her money.

Her first intent had been to keep running. She dumped Brick's Honda in a box-store parking lot, tracked down a cheap old Ford she could buy for cash from a private party, holed up in a roadside motel, drastically cut and dyed her hair. She was ready to resume driving south . . . but then decided on a change of plan.

She was sure Rybus had come up with the ransom money. So it was clear to her: Theo had kept the money. It all made sense. It would be exactly the kind of devious thing he would have concocted.

Maybe it was even part of a larger scheme to overthrow his boss. How he planned to get away with taking a million dollars of Yancey's money, she wasn't quite sure, but she was convinced that was exactly what he was doing.

She wasn't going to let him get away with that. She could deal with the likelihood he had killed Brick by now, but he had betrayed her not once but twice, and that was unforgivable.

She stopped at a second-hand store and purchased a set of military camouflage fatigues, a matching cap, and a pair of huge dark wraparound sunglasses like an old lady with eye cataracts would wear. She figured with her junky car, close-cropped bleached hair and the outfit, nobody would recognize her. She would be safe enough returning to the city. She knew all of Theo's haunts, even the ones he kept secret from the crew. She could cruise around until she found him, shadow him to somewhere quiet and deserted, and deal with him.

One of the few things that had never left her possession was the Glock automatic in her bag. That would likely come in handy.

And thus she now found herself furtively cruising up and down various side streets of the city, eyes constantly moving behind those gigantic sunglasses, on the lookout for that familiar Navigator. She had been driving for four or five hours now, an almost-depleted bag of hamburgers and fries from a drive-through on the seat beside her. Maybe this was crazy; the longer she was out here, the more the chance that she might be spotted or something else might happen. It began to seem that her original course of action was indeed the better one: drive out of here, get on the freeway, and head as far away as she could get.

She couldn't believe her luck when she saw the Lincoln Navigator a half block ahead, pulling into the underground driveway of a building that was familiar to her. No question. It was him.

'Bingo,' she whispered to herself, cocking her finger like a gun. 'Gotcha now.'

She pulled over to wait.

★   ★   ★

Yancey Rybus was not particularly a fan of the big sport-utility vehicles favored by many in his crew. He could understand the usefulness of a large-capacity high-performance vehicle with heavily tinted windows, but the trade-off was a car that stood out like a sore thumb to all the wrong people. Usually he favored one of his two low-key Lexus sedans, but today he was being driven by Tiny, who fit into a very limited number of vehicles, so they were cruising the streets in his pearl-grey Cadillac Escalade. As it was, Tiny barely wedged into the spacious seat when it was moved all the way back. Rybus sat impassively in the passenger seat while scanning the streets and speaking tersely into his phone. Between short conversations with various members of the crew who were also on the look for T.C., he would give directions to Tiny.

'Circle around the block again. Keep your eyes peeled for his Navigator. Maybe he'll return to the Shafford house that the lad Nate told us about.'

Tiny, a man of few words, nodded and continued to slowly drive up and down the streets, looking right and left.

★   ★   ★

Theo took the time to drive around the block a couple of times, scouting out things with care. The houses on this stretch of Shafford were quite similar: close together but with room for a driveway that led to a garage or, in many cases, to a converted back unit.

Theo's addled brain was in overdrive. It couldn't be a coincidence that this Musgrave dude lived just up the block from where Lydia and Big Red had been holed up. Obviously Musgrave had to be in on the whole thing, a skilled manipulator in his own right. He was living a very sly double life; the park ranger job or whatever, all that nature and nice-guy stuff, had to have been a front, a job allowing him to slide in through the park and take the money while Big Red distracted the crew and led them away.

Then again, maybe Big Red was just a

clueless pigeon in this whole thing. Realizing how devious his old girlfriend really was, that started to make real sense to Theo. Big Red was telling the truth when he said he thought there was no money. Lydia had been planning to dump him and run off with the other guy all along.

The question now was: where was Musgrave? Did he still have the money? Had he fled with Lydia, or was he still here?

He pulled up into the driveway of the address, scoping out the main house. He had just gotten out of his Navigator when the door flew open and a very large middle-aged woman stormed out onto the stoop.

'That's private property!' she hollered in a deep voice. 'Get yourself out of there right now!'

Theo, now in a presentable white shirt and jeans, was ready to play the nice guy still again. He spread his hands in a helpless gesture and smiled sheepishly. 'I'm sorry, ma'am, really. I'll back right out of here right now and park on the street. I was just looking for my friend Webster. Webster Musgrave?'

The lady hitched a husky thumb back towards the rear of the property, making the roll of fat on her arm shake. 'He's my tenant, in the back house. But get that car out of my driveway first!'

'Absolutely, ma'am. My apologies.' Maybe Musgrave was still there after all. Theo stepped back into his car, noting that the scowling woman wasn't buying any of his charm, and backed out. Too bad: he wanted his car off the street so it wouldn't be seen easily. He drove around the corner to the parking lot of a large supermarket, the Food Extravaganza, figuring it wouldn't stand out there like it would on the street, and hustled back on foot.

Felix stepped out from behind a tree across the street and crossed to meet Theo. This was a tough block in which to remain inconspicuous, too residential and open. Theo indicated with a nod of his head to follow him down the driveway.

'Park somewhere safe?' he murmured as Felix caught up with him.

186

'Behind a building two blocks away. I'm not liking this, T.C. Any time now Nate's liable to lead them over to that other house and we could be spotted.'

'I've got to take that chance. The money might still be here. It's the only shot we've got, or else we're as good as dead.'

The back house was a similar garage conversion to the one where they had confronted Big Red. There was a light shining inside but no apparent activity. They peered through the front windows and finally Theo knocked on the door. There was no answer.

Like the other unit, there was no other way in or out. There was no back door. The structure backed up against a fence and had minimal clearance with other fences to either side.

'So what do we do?' asked Felix.

'We go in.'

Felix shrugged. 'Wish I'd known to bring my picks.'

'Wait a minute.' Theo had stepped on the old rubber doormat on the stoop and felt a bump. He lifted the mat and picked up a key on a silver fob shaped like a turtle. 'Looks like Web plans on coming back. Nice of him to leave this in plain sight.'

This was not, he reasoned, a good sign. You didn't leave a million dollars locked up in a house and leave the key under the mat, did you? It was still his only hope.

Once inside, he pulled the door locked shut behind them and closed the blinds. It didn't look like the place had been vacated; it was still what one would call 'lived-in.' In fact it was a downright pigsty. This Webster dude was a real slob. Theo, who prided himself on being fastidious, shook his head in contempt. Sloppy life, sloppy thinking. What kind of incompetent fools had Lydia picked up here?

They commenced turning the place upside down. After exhausting obvious places like drawers or closets, Felix started pulling back the threadbare rugs and checking for loose floorboards. They knocked on all the walls, looking for hollows. After over an hour of going over the small unit, they had found nothing.

Felix, still mystified at exactly what was going on, wiped his profusely sweating forehead and shook his head in bewilderment.

Theo sat down on the couch but hardly looked relaxed. His knee kept bobbing up and down and he kept muttering things, not always intelligibly; Felix began to worry about his state of mind. 'This guy's got the money,' Theo repeated over and over. 'I'm sure of it. He must have it.'

Felix tried to get him to focus. 'So what's our next move?'

'Let's wait a while. Nobody's going to see us here. Go put this key back under the mat. Maybe we'll get lucky and our boy Webster will turn up.'

Felix's massive body ebbed and flowed in a gigantic sigh. He put out his hand. 'Okay, you got it. And then maybe you can bring me up to speed on why we're here?'

It was not a comfortable wait period. Felix was getting truly concerned as he listened to Theo's rambling explanation, and the long agitated silence that followed was just as unnerving. Theo couldn't sit still and kept getting up and pacing, looking through the blinds. Finally, with still another glance at his watch, he said, 'It's past four. We can't just wait here. We gotta go.'

'Where we gonna go, T.C.?'

'I don't know. Let me think this out.' They walked out the door, locking it and leaving the key back under the mat, and headed out towards Shafford. Theo kept talking quietly to himself, his head down, as they walked.

'We gotta find this guy. I know he's got the money. I know he's the key. We're not going to find Lydia, but . . .'

Suddenly Theo felt Felix's heavy arm across his chest, bringing him to an abrupt halt, since Felix had also just come to a full stop.

'Hey, what . . .'

They had almost reached the sidewalk, and in front of them, in the middle of Shafford Avenue, stood a woman.

At least Theo thought she was a woman. She was wearing baggy camouflage fatigues and cap and a pair of huge, ridiculous-looking wraparound dark glasses. Her hair under the cap was tennis-ball short and bright yellow. Her legs were spread in a low-gravity stance and she held, in a two-hand grip, what looked like a 9mm Glock, pointed at them, shifting back and forth between Felix and Theo.

'What the hell?' Theo said.

'Stay right there, both of you!' she yelled, continuing to shift the pistol back and forth between them. 'Not a step closer!'

'Lydia?' Theo said, unbelieving.

'Where's my money, you rat? I want my money that you stole!'

'Wait a minute.' Theo raised his hands placatingly and, he hoped, not threateningly. '*Your* money? That *I* stole? Don't you mean Yancey's money that *you* stole? You and your new boyfriend Webster?'

'Who's Webster? What are you talking about? Why are you even here, coming out of this house? I know you found our place down the street, but why here?'

Now both Felix and Theo had their hands raised and were trying to take slow baby steps to get closer to the lunatic woman in camos with the gun. She yelled

191

once more, 'Not one step closer! I *will* kill you both!'

There was suddenly a loud squeal as a pearl-grey Cadillac Escalade slid several inches on dry pavement and screeched to a halt a foot in front of Lydia. The two front doors flew open. From the driver's side un-wedged a mountainous figure familiar to all of them, so big he even dwarfed Felix: the man they knew as Tiny.

From the passenger side, Yancey Rybus stepped down. He slammed his car door.

Lydia swiveled her weapon around, and somehow it discharged, the bullet smacking into the front of the car. It would never really be adequately decided whether it was an intentional or accidental shot, but clearly it did cause everybody to move. In moments, there were five people facing down one another on the street, everyone with weapons drawn.

Webster's landlady, who had been blissfully unaware of everything that had been transpiring, heard the tire screech and walked out her door just in time for Lydia's gun to fire. She let loose a banshee scream at the top of her lungs and ran back inside, slamming the door.

For an agonizingly long stretch, the five stood their ground, all in firing stances, pistols in two-hand grips with locked elbows, nervously shifting their aims back and forth at each other like twitchy insects. Sooner or later something was going to give.

'Hold it!' came a voice from the sidewalk. Everybody momentarily turned to see a guy in a rumpled sports coat and pants, also wielding a sidearm, in much the same pose as the rest of them, except he seemed to be gasping for breath.

'Who the hell are you?' yelled Theo, Felix and Tiny almost in unison.

The reply came out in almost a wheeze. 'I'm a cop. Detective Marlon Morrison, Personal Crimes. Now everybody lower your weapons and let's sort this out!'

'Man,' laughed Felix, 'if you the po-lice, you the saddest, tiredest-looking po-lice I ever saw.'

'You're damned right I'm sad and tired,' Marlon boomed. 'And angry. *And* in the worst mood I may just *ever* have been in, and none of that is good news for any of you, because I might just lose my temper and start dropping you all without concern for the inquest that'll follow! You all look like you know guns, so you can see I've got a standard police-issue Glock with fifteen rounds here — that's three for each of you — and I've got top proficiency rating on the range! So start lowering those weapons *now*!'

The fact of the matter was that Marlon had not visited the police shooting range in years. It was lucky he bothered to clean his service weapon now and then. He hoped his speech sounded more convincing to them than it did to him.

Oddly, it did give them all a moment's pause, but nobody lowered their guns. It was a tense, dark comedy, six people in spread-legged stance, shifting their aims back and forth at each other in telegraphed stage motions. It dragged on and on.

It was Rybus who spoke first, his unruffled voice cutting through the tension of the moment. 'Hello, T.C. If I didn't know better, I'd swear you've been avoiding me.'

'I can explain everything, Yancey. She's got your money. Her and her boyfriend.'

Lydia exploded, still shifting her pistol back and forth nervously. 'I don't have any money and you know it! And he wasn't my boyfriend! You killed him, didn't you?'

'I'm not talking about Big Red. You know who I mean. The other guy.'

'Wait a minute,' Rybus said. 'Lydia? T.C., here I thought you had cut her loose!' He actually laughed. 'This is all beginning to make a lot of sense to me now.'

'What other guy?' Lydia yelled at Theo. 'What are you talking about?'

'The three of you were in this together, to swipe the dog and take the money!'

'Three? There was me and Brick — that was it! Have you gone nuts?'

'Yes,' hissed Rybus. 'A great deal of sense. This is a nice little charade you two are pulling. All this fiction about a big red-haired guy and losing the money and all. T.C., I am very disappointed in you.'

'Big Red was real!' shouted Theo. 'I killed him last night!'

195

'I knew it!' screamed Lydia. 'Now you're making up some fake story and some other fake guy so you can take the money and run off yourself!'

'You're all sounding fake to me,' said Rybus, still calm despite his rigid locked-arm firing stance.

'Would somebody say something that makes some sense?' demanded a very tired Marlon Morrison. 'Or better yet, could we all just put down the weapons and we'll resolve this without anybody getting shot?' He realized that time was not on his side. A bunch of angry, apparently insane gangsters with big guns . . . and him. Every second made it more likely something bad was going to happen. He wondered if his amazing luck of the day had finally run out.

He heard more squeals of tires as vehicles came hard around the corners at either end of the block. He looked around to see the blinking lights of several police cruisers and even a van. In moments they were surrounded by black and white vehicles, doors flying open and disgorging officers in flak vests and heavy ordnance.

The gangsters may have been insane but they weren't stupid. Weapons were dropped and hands were raised. His day, Marlon realized with immense relief, had stayed lucky.

10

By the time Marlon got home that night, he was so exhausted that he collapsed into bed without eating or even undressing, and slept a solid twelve hours. His luck held true for the next few days. From the moment she was brought into the station, Lydia began talking. She accused Theo of murdering her accomplice, the man she called Brick. She immediately sought deals from the District Attorney's office in exchange for telling pretty much anything and everything she knew about the Rybus organization — which as the recent girlfriend to its second in command, she promised, was substantial. The prosecutor's office was very interested.

That was how Marlon finally put together the whole story about Lydia, Brixton, and the dognapping of Rybus's beloved pit bull Vanessa.

There were sufficient grounds to hold everybody long enough that they were still in custody when forensic evidence began to arrive. The older body found with Bradley Brixton had been identified as Wallace Barnes, a former associate of Yancey Rybus. Ballistics matched the bullets found in both Barnes and Darius Mitchell to the very weapon possessed by Sylvester Faamoana, better known to his own associates as Tiny, on the afternoon of his apprehension on Shafford Avenue. The slugs found in the body of Bradley Brixton were a match to the Desert Eagle semi-automatic belonging to Theo Charles.

Forensics matched fingerprints found in the car stolen from Luis Molino to the murdered Bradley Brixton. But there was more. Numerous other prints would be matched to one Barry Grimes, who turned out to be still another member of the Rybus organization. One thing just kept leading to another.

Further excavation of the hillside dump ground gradually yielded three more bodies, in various states of decay. It was clear that the neglected site had been a convenient drop-off for murder victims for some time now. The news caused a media sensation, with city officials scrambling on camera to express shocked outrage and promising a thorough investigation and cleanup. Ultimately all three victims would be identified as former associates of the Rybus organization and their murders tied to 'Tiny' Faamoana through diligent efforts by the SID and coroner.

There was sufficient fallout that Rybus and his cronies would not be offered bail and would be looking forward to lots of court time. It was not only the city that had become interested in the information Lydia had to offer; state and federal agencies were perking up their ears and preparing their own cases. Rybus and his crew remained stolid, observing the code of their culture in hard silence. The only thing heard from Rybus were complaints that he missed his dog Vanessa. Expensive defense teams were being assembled for a spate of drawn-out legal battles.

Nothing would probably be decided, Marlon figured, before he had actually retired. That was okay; at least a bunch of them were off the street for the foreseeable future. In the meantime, Rybus's vaunted organization was in a state of chaos. There would be players scrambling for position, violently striving to fill the vacuum and re-establish order with themselves at the top. In the end, he realized, that would not be a totally good thing. Personal Crimes would have its share of new violent crimes.

Marlon hoped that Lydia wouldn't get off completely free despite her deals. It was one of the things he hated most about his job: as often as not, the guilty went unpunished, or were dealt nothing more than a slap on the wrist. He figured she'd be fielding offers for a book and movie deal before she ever left custody.

This whole experience certainly hadn't made him any less of a cynic.

Marlon had scored a coup that would carry him for many months to come, if he so chose to ride it. For a while, there wouldn't be much of an issue made of the pile of open cases still on his desk. He had a pass to sit back indefinitely, and he gave it a lot of thought in the ensuing weeks. It was tempting.

Something else happened to make him think about it differently. It was the afternoon that Hank Castillo called him into his office, put his own paperwork aside, and actually invited him to sit down. This was generally unheard of in the Lou's domain.

'Marlon, I have to tell you frankly, I wasn't sure you had something like this in you anymore. You surprised me. You surprised a lot of us.'

Marlon knew that. The other detectives of the Personal Crimes Unit had each extended their own congratulations to him already. Some were more diplomatic than others, but the underlying message was consistent: we didn't think you had it in you anymore.

'Thanks, Lou. A lot of it was just dumb luck.' Marlon was feeling magnanimous these days and it wasn't about being humble; it was about hating to be in the spotlight. He accepted he might be something of a shirker, averse to attention, but he also wasn't a braggart.

Castillo smiled under his thick salt-and-pepper mustache. The man was unbelievably distinguished-looking, Marlon reflected; never a hair out of place or a spot on one of his white shirts. 'There's always luck involved, but there was a lot of excellent police work done here too. That, and just plain grinding footwork. I'm proud of you, Marlon. I've recommended a citation for you.'

Marlon didn't really want that. A bonus check, maybe; even a raise, sure. But he knew the city and the department were too strapped and perhaps too stingy to go that far. He guessed he'd have to look forward to a day when he would have to drag his ceremonial uniform out of the back of his closet and stand uncomfortably under a bunch of lights while a deputy chief handed him a plaque. There were worse things to have to undergo. For instance, he could have been shot multiple times by five gangsters on Shafford Avenue.

Gene Hogan made several calls to Marlon over the next few days, trying to pick his brain for information relating to his own drug cases, which had been aided

203

immeasurably by recent events. Gene's own inertia need not be interrupted; Personal Crimes had done a good job of sweeping the streets for him. Marlon remained courteous but not overly helpful. All relevant information would be available to the entire department soon enough.

Hogan made overtures to get together with his old partner and just hash over good old times. Marlon simply said he'd think about it.

Several wildly disparate versions of the story of the dognapping and the money drop emerged; nobody would ever totally make sense of what had really happened. The money remained the biggest mystery. Everybody accused somebody else of running off with it, and there seemed to be no hard evidence whatsoever for any explanation. Marlon's favorite personal theory was that Lydia had the money and planned to return one day to reclaim it from wherever she had salted it away. That would explain her eager cooperation with the authorities. But then again, maybe Theo had kept the money and never actually dropped it off. That was certainly a possibility; he might be holding out hope to someday be paroled. To a hardened gangster, a cool million was worth doing time for.

The only other person to have even conceivably made contact with the money — or not — had taken his knowledge to the grave. Marlon struggled to make sense of the different stories he heard about the victim he knew as Bradley Brixton, who he came to realize was the same person Lydia called Brick and Theo Charles called Big Red. He figured it would ultimately all get figured out but not by him; it still confused him mightily.

Theo's claims of a mysterious man named Web seemed preposterous to Marlon. He never even bothered to follow up on it.

11

One last question remains: what *did* happen to Webster Musgrave? What *did* happen to the box of money?

Earlier Wednesday morning, after finally getting several hours of sorely needed sleep and feeling as if his head and stomach were back to normal, Webster sat at the kitchenette table in his tiny back house on Shafford Avenue and considered his next move. Passing the hundred-dollar bill had apparently gone well. His overwhelming obsession with the box of money seemed to have passed, at least to the point that he could now think rationally about what to do next, and he had achieved some clarity about his plans.

He was going to keep the money.

There was no way he could return it safely or to the benefit of anybody who wasn't a criminal. Maybe that was a rationalization, but so be it. If he continued to act carefully, he ought to be able to spend the money in frugal and discreet ways. He needed to think of himself not as a sudden millionaire, but perhaps as someone who'd acquired a decent job that would pay him well over the long run. He needed the money, but he didn't need a lavish lifestyle; if he went on living pretty much the way he always had, this money could last him for years to come. He might have to move to someplace remote, but he was confident that he could come up with the right plan.

Now to involve Evangeline in this.

He had decided he couldn't tell her about the money, not yet, possibly not ever. That might become difficult if they got married — and they could do that now — and they occupied the same house. Even if he got a new well-paying job as a cover, that wouldn't fool her for very long. Sooner or later he'd have to own up to the truth. But not right away. He'd figure this out one step at a time.

Evangeline might not warm immediately to the idea of moving away from the city. Maybe he could come up with a job in a small town or rural area as an excuse. He'd make it all work.

The first thing was to start dropping hints to her. She wouldn't be coming home from her parents' for another week, and they had only had sporadic contact since she had left. Web realized he hadn't contacted her since this whole affair with the money had started. He had been too busy, or too distracted, to even check his email for the past few days.

His laptop sat on the kitchen table. He popped it open and booted it up, listening to the full BONG tone that filled his cramped little kitchenette.

When he opened his email window, he noted that he had four new messages, and three were from Evangeline. The first, from midday Monday, around the time Web was getting drunk in the park, simply read 'Sweetie, we have to talk. You're not picking up your phone. Call me please.'

The second, from early Tuesday morning, when Web was contemplating his box of money through his insomniac blear, read, 'Web, we REALLY need to talk. I've tried your phone and you're not picking up. Please call me. It's important.'

Web pulled his phone out of his pocket and realized he had turned it off while drinking at the park Monday and had never thought to turn it back on. He did so now and found nine voicemails from Evangeline over the past forty-eight hours. They were all terse requests to please call her, in an urgent voice.

Her third and final email had come through this morning.

Dearest Webster,

This is very hard for me to write but I can't get hold of you to talk. I owe you better than this, and I am truly sorry.

I told you I came to Buffalo to see my parents, and that is partly true. But I also came here for another reason. Over the past few months I have reconnected with my high school boyfriend, Kurt, and decided to meet up with him in person and see if what I suspected was true, that the old chemistry was still there. Without trying to be mean, I have to say it was, and even more than I had suspected.

We have decided to try to make it together. Kurt has a decent job here as regional sales manager for Clips, the office supply chain. He would be able to support us both and we could start a family. I'm sorry, Web, I care for you deeply but I do not see any way that we could ever have a family if we were together, and it means everything to me to be able to. I also have to wonder if the spark we once felt for one another is still there. Our communication lately hasn't been all that great. It's as if we've just been going through the motions in recent weeks. Perhaps you've come to feel the same as I do, that it's time to move on.

What I'm trying to say is, I am not going to be returning. I gave up the lease on my apartment and have already arranged to have my things shipped here to Buffalo. I'm sorry for devastating you in this way but I hope one day you can forgive me. You are a wonderful man with a big heart and I hope you find the way to care for the animals you love for the rest of a happy life.

Love,
Evangeline

Webster sat very still for a long time. He had experienced a momentary shock but now, he was surprised to realize, he felt . . . nothing. He wasn't devastated. He wasn't even sad.

What he felt was more like relief.

Evangeline was possibly right. Maybe they had both been ready to move on and hadn't been willing to admit it. In fact he had just been contemplating how hard it would be to do something vital to a relationship: be honest. He had been planning how to scam her, building a regular tower of lies. That should have been be a warning sign.

It actually shamed him, but his major thought now was how much less complicated things had suddenly become.

He selected the fourth and final email, which had also come through this morning.

211

Dear Webster,

You might remember me from a conversation we had several months ago while I was visiting the Aquatic Bird Sanctuary Park facilities with my group, the Downstate Desert Conservancy. I was struck by your deep affinity for the wildlife in the park and your obvious sense of duty to protect it. At the time I mentioned we might need people such as yourself at the Conservancy, and you had expressed some interest if conditions were right.

We have just opened a position as one of the head curators for the Conservancy, a three hundred square mile desert space that is the home to multiple species of tortoises, lizards, hares, vultures, and many other animals. Your job would be to survey the entire area regularly and to oversee the preservation of the desert environment and its denizens.

It would require your moving here to the desert, and let me tell you, it's desolate. But it's not totally uncivilized: there's a small town, Crystalline, with amenities like supermarkets, banks, movie theatres and so forth, and some of the nicest people you could hope to have as neighbors and friends. We have a library, a movie theater and internet service, and some very intelligent and creative people who have come here to escape the insanity of the big city. I'm afraid the pay is quite low since we're a public nonprofit. To be frank, I suppose this isn't exactly a glowing career opportunity. But I can pretty much guarantee that, if you apply, you will get the position, and I can also guarantee that from what I know about you, you would absolutely love it.

Please let me know as soon as you can.
Best wishes,
Callista Weintraub,
Downstate Desert Conservancy

This, Web considered, would take serious thought.

The serious thought lasted about three minutes.

An hour later he had his car packed and had replied to Callista, telling her to hold the position, and he'd be down to talk to her.

He took a couple of the hundred-dollar bills out of the box and sealed the rest up with a roll of packing tape he had bought yesterday at Clips. He wondered how many rolls of that tape old Kurt had sold, and wished Evangeline well with her new/old, staid middle-management boyfriend.

Time to throw caution to the wind, Web told himself. He didn't care about the rest of the stuff he left behind. His rent was paid through the end of the month and then the landlady could have everything. He even left a light on. He locked up his house and left the keys under the mat, then carried the box of money to the car and stuck it way back in his trunk. Maybe it wouldn't make the trip, and he'd show up in the desert with no money and having to somehow make a go of it. Maybe somebody would catch up with him en route and he'd never even make it to the desert.

Or maybe, just maybe, he'd make it safely and live happily ever after in Crystalline among the tortoises and the hares.

It was worth the shot. As the old song went, 'Freedom's just another word for nothing left to lose.'

He started the engine and backed the car out of the driveway from the back house. For the first time in several days, he had a smile on his face.